A Crush for the Holidays

E.L. OUGH

A Crush for the Holidays

Copyright © 2024 by E.L. Ough

All rights reserved.

Cover Art by Regitse Liljadorff

Alpha Reading by A.E. Jensen and Regitse Liljadorff

Beta Reading by Mariansen PA

Editing & Formatting by Jenn ReadsBooks

Cover and subtitle fonts: Creative Fabrica

For birthday girl Jenn
For being the most fancee beyotch ever.
This book is for your Canadian arse.

Author's Note

A Crush for the Holidays is an MM romance published as part of *Home for the Holidays*, a collection of standalone novellas connected by a singular theme: spreading queer joy during the holiday season. For more titles, please see the *Home for the Holidays* list at the back of the book.

While I don't (personally) think there are any triggers in this story, please note Tristan's mother suffers from dementia and no longer recognises him when he comes to visit.

What You Can Expect:
*Cabin in the forest
*Only One Bed
*Forced Proximity
*Sassy Brat
*Best-friend's-dad
*Secret Crush
*The Shortest Shorts
*Cardigan Hotness
*Snowed In
*Pearling
*Dress Up

Please note:

As the author of this book is British, please expect 'British-isms,' different spellings to reflect said Britishness, and lots of British humour.

Chapter One

"Oh Tris, you're just the person I was looking for. You got a sec?" my boss Jeb says, walking past me in the hallway, just as I'm leaving the dining room.

"Yeah, course. What's up?"

"Let's go into the office."

I follow him down the hallway until we reach the last door. I work for Halfway House, a literal house that acts as a shelter for the unhoused, five days a week. Jeb and his wife established the place after Jeb's brother passed away while living as a homeless person. Since he couldn't help his brother in conquering his addiction, he resolved to lend a hand to others experiencing homelessness and/or addiction in his brother's name. After inheriting a lump sum from his grandmother, Jeb and his wife, Elise, sold their property and purchased an old, eight-bedroom house.

The house has become a sanctuary for homeless individuals, offering them not only hot meals, showers, and medical help but also a few hours of respite and safety. Jeb and Elise used to occupy the top floor, but as the house became more crowded with new people dropping in each day, they made the choice to move to a smaller house down the street with their newborn daughter, Dolly.

The office we walk into is situated at the back of the building on the bottom floor. It's a small yet charming space with ample natural light streaming through the large windows, offering a view of the beautiful garden outside. "Have a seat, Tris."

I plant myself on the green plastic garden chair across from him. Jeb and Elise are total hippies—dreads and all, and they dress like they just raided their grandma's closet. They only buy second-hand clothes. It's commendable. I have so much love for both of them; they have the biggest hearts and are such wonderful human beings. That's why I find so much joy in working here.

"So," Jeb says, sitting across from me with a file that clearly has my name on the front. "Holiday."

"*Agh*, you know I don't want it," I complain.

"It's not a matter of wanting it or not, but you have to take it, or you'll lose it."

"But I don't need a week off. Can't you just put me down as taking the time off and I'll just work the week, anyway?" I smile endearingly, hoping he agrees.

"No can do. You know that's not how this works. It's one week, Tris."

"Except it's not. It's one week off for my annual holiday, then another week because I'm not scheduled back on till after Christmas," I counter.

What the hell am I gonna do for two entire weeks? *Fourteen* days.

"Sorry Tris," he laughs. "But you work just as hard as Elise and me. You seriously need a break. We love you and don't want you to burn out. I don't think you've had a single day off since you started here a year ago. You even came in when you were sick, remember?" He raises an eyebrow at me. Yeah, I'd tried to fake it, pretending I didn't have a fever.

Well, he's definitely won this argument. I can't help that I love my job. I enjoy meeting new people and listening to their stories. I feel like I'm wanted here. Needed. You can always find something to do, whether it's pitching in with cooking and serving food or offering new tents and clothes to individuals on their first visit. This place has such a great atmosphere, you never know what surprises the day will bring, and the staff here are the most down-to-earth people you'll ever meet.

I slump in the chair, folding my arms across my chest, and let out a deep sigh. "Who's gonna handle things here during Christmas? It's just over a week away. I'm sure you could use some help."

"We've got it all covered. The kitchen staff is on rotation. Maggie and Ross are in charge when Elise and I are off duty. We have two locum doctors on call. We're all set, Tris. It's Dolly's first Christmas," he says, a smile that can only be described as that of a proud dad on his face. "So even we're taking some time off."

"Fine," I grumble under my breath. "When does it start?" Please say 2033.

"As soon as you finish work today. I don't wanna see you until January third." Jeb raises his eyebrows, waiting for me to acknowledge him in some way.

"Okay, jeez. I won't come back." Shit, maybe I can buy one of those disguises and pretend to be a new intern or some shit like that? Just sneak right in. '*Hi, I'm Don! I'm here for the intern position.*'

"Good, now go finish your shift. I heard Trixy was looking for you."

Ah, my lovely Trixy, a woman of sixty-eight who has spent nearly two decades on the streets. Her marriage crumbled, and with no children or family to turn to, she ultimately ended up homeless. She's bloody amazing. Every week, she tells me stories that either have me laughing or crying. She loves to crochet, saying it helps her pass the time while she indulges in her favourite hobby of people-watching. Give her thirty seconds, and she'll quickly determine if someone possesses a good character or not.

We supply her with wool, and she churns out these god-awful hats for the House. They're part of the care packages we provide to new arrivals. I've got one too. It comprises a mishmash of colours that go with absolutely nothing in my wardrobe. Ugly as fuck, yet it's one of my most prized possessions because Trixy made it for me. She said it's bursting with colour, just like me. So, if you see folks in London strolling around with ugly hats, you can bet they came from her.

Once I've left Jeb's office, I set out to find my girl and give her the wool I purchased from *Hobbycraft*. Yeah, I know, but it's not exactly like I've got someone special at home to spend all my hard-earned money on and until I do—if that ever happens—I'll splurge on top-notch wool for my girl Trixy.

Chapter Two

"So, Daxy. I've been thinking."

Little did Jason know, one use of a nickname would have dire consequences for him. I do *not* like nicknames, and I already know where this is heading. We're on our third date. We met at the primary school where I work. He was just a temp, but we hit it off immediately. He was covering a class because another staff member had a stomachache. Cue the eye roll. Grab an *Imodium* and tough it out like the rest of us.

Anyway, we started talking during lunch break and I thought he looked cute in his beige trousers and crisp white shirt. I should have known right then. Beige is boring and reliable, but not fun.

We had a good time on the first date. The second date went even better, and he was amazing in bed. But this third date is going where they all end up. In the bin.

Even after clearly stating to Jason that I am not interested in anything serious or long-term or anything that requires more than a few hours of my time, he still hasn't got the message. Judging from the tone of his voice, he believes he has convinced me to change for him. Well, I have news. It's not happening.

With a forced smile, I ask him while finishing my beer. "What's that then?"

"Well, we've been getting along so incredibly well these past few dates that I feel like I know every little detail about you already." Jason bats his stupid eyelashes. I'm salty that he's ruined my evening. "Now, I know you said you don't do relationships," his tone is slightly pleading, an edge of hopefulness to it I instantly want to squish under my foot. "But I believe we've got something special here."

And there it is.

I hold in the sigh and clench my fist under the table. Why can't I just go on dates and hook up without having to be in a committed relationship? They're not my cup of tea. Been there, done that, got the T-shirt. Do not rate. Why is it so hard to get your dick wet these days? Like suck it and move on.

Jason reaches out to hold my hand across the table. However, I'm familiar with this move; they believe holding my hand will magically alter my thoughts. It won't, no matter how hard you try. I move my hand aside and gesture to the waiter for the bill.

Such a shame, because it was a great meal. I ordered the steak, while Jason opted for the salmon salad. He paired his meal with a glass of white wine, while I had a beer. It was pleasant. Jason, with his cute appearance and blond hair perfectly styled to the side with just the right amount of gel. The navy shirt complemented his *beige* trousers nicely. I was looking forward to pounding his ass tonight. Now I'm going home to use my hand. Sad times.

"Look Jason, you're a really nice guy, but this just isn't going to work out. It's me, not you." That good old line. Make them think you're the problem, not them.

"Oh, don't be like that. You just need a bit more time. That's okay. I don't mind waiting."

You'll be waiting a long time then. I order him an *Uber* since I drove my car here. I know I'm being a cunt by not driving him home, but I'm over it. Chivalry is dead, ladies and gentlemen.

With a smile, I pay the cute waiter and leave a generous tip before getting up to leave. In a fluster, Jason trails after me.

"Dax, come on. I'm sorry. I know I come on too strong, forgive me. Let's go back to yours and we can talk about it."

Thankfully, his Uber pulls up. "Thank you for your company tonight," I lean in and kiss his cheek, "but we won't be seeing each other again. So do yourself a favour and lose my number." I pull open the car door for him, not because I'm a gentleman, but because I just want to hurry this along.

"You're an arsehole," he says with a huff, getting into the cab.

Never said I wasn't. I slam the door, walking over to my *BMW* to drive myself back home. To my house. My nice, big, *empty* house.

Walking through the door, I hear the jingle of my keys as they land on the kitchen counter, and I immediately head to the fridge to grab a cold beer. Another night gone to shit because people don't listen.

The piercing sound of my alarm clock startles me awake. 8 A.M. on a Saturday morning.

My routine has been the same for the past 6 years, ever since Jake, my son, went off to university. He is currently pursuing a medical degree and thoroughly enjoying the university experience. Juggling his studies, hospital shifts, and quality time with his boyfriend, Lewis, doesn't leave us with a lot of time for family stuff, but we make it work. We have a video call every Saturday, and he sends me text messages throughout the week. Once a month, we gather at my place for family night, and even my ex, his mum, joins us.

Jenny and I crossed paths at university, where we were both pursuing our dreams of becoming teachers. Our schedules aligned perfectly, and we ended up in every single class together. We were drawn to each other, and we found comfort and joy in our friendship. However, as time went on and the demands of university consumed us, dating became too overwhelming for us both. We had already been spending all our time together, so transitioning into a romantic relationship seemed like the logical next step.

A few fumbles later, and she was pregnant. Talk about throwing a spanner in the works. Yet again, we found a way to make it work.

With my parents' wealth, I enjoyed a privileged upbringing, for which I'm grateful. However, becoming a young father was not the path they had in mind for me. Additionally, they were not happy when we decided not to marry, but Jenny and I eventually decided that we were better off remaining friends.

Jenny is the only girl I've ever slept with, and it wasn't mind-blowing for either of us. It was only after I became interested in a guy on the football team that I realised I was gay. Mother dearest, not wanting her reputation as a parent to be tarnished among her snobby friends, generously contributed to our purchase of this house when Jake was born so we could live together as a family.

Throwing off my cover, I get up and stretch. God, I'm getting old. I'm sure my body never used to crack this much. I put on my glasses, straighten the bed, and take a quick detour to the bathroom before heading to the kitchen to make a cup of coffee.

I quickly pick up my *iPad* and prop it up on the kitchen counter as I toss some bread into the toaster. When it rings, I answer and am greeted by Jake's smiling face. "Hey, son. How're things?"

"Ah, you know, busy. I had a full week at the hospital. I'm tired as heck, but I love it."

His warm smile reaches his eyes. "Oh, I have some news. Lewis's mum invited us to go stay with her for the week... in Paris! Can you believe it? So, I get to relax before it all starts again after Christmas."

"Well, that's nice. How the other half lives, eh?" I laugh. Jake deserves a break; he works so hard, and one day soon, he'll be a qualified doctor. We're so proud of him for following his dream career. "Where's Lewis?"

"He's packing for us now; you know I'm terrible at it." We both laugh. Yeah, I do. The one time Jenny and I asked Jake to pack his own case for a family trip to Florida at age fifteen, thinking he was old enough to start doing things for himself, turned out to be too much of an ask. Jake ended up bringing three pairs of joggers and two hoodies in 40-degree heat because he'd forgotten that he might need anything else. He'd been too busy reading a medical book the night before and forgotten to pack till the last minute.

"Yeah, I remember," I smile.

"So, Dad, what's the plan for the run-up to Christmas? Got any hot dates lined up? How many have you had this week?" he asks with a smirk because my son knows about my terrible dating history.

"Cheeky sod! I've only had one this week, but this guy..." I trail off.

"Wait, don't tell me! He thought he was '*the one*?' How dare he!"

I sigh, pushing back my messy brown hair. "Yeah, something like that."

"You've gotta be running outta guys," Jake chuckles. "There has to be someone who can make my dear old dad weak in the knees."

Oh, they make my knees weak. That's not the problem; it's the rest of it. Once Jenny and I agreed to remain friends and co-parent Jake, they both became my top priority. Juggling between university and raising a child, I found myself with little time for anything else. By the time Jake left for university and Jenny moved out, I had become set in my ways. I like my own company, my own space, my routine. That's why Saturday's my cleaning day. I dust and vacuum every corner of the house, from top to bottom, change my bed, and do all the laundry. Then I go food shopping for the week and end up ordering Indian takeout, grabbing a cold beer, and watching a movie. On weekdays, I work at Kingslee Primary School, where I've been for the past ten years. And once or twice a week I try to get laid.

Fun, with no commitment. Although, lately, I've been wondering if I'm truly having fun or if I'm just kidding myself.

"You know how I am Jake; I think my time for settling down has been and gone."

"That's rubbish and you know it. You're only forty-two. You're just scared. Don't be afraid to start over, Dad."

Wise words coming from my son. "Don't you try to use your sweet-talking doctor skills on your old man! Save them for Lewis and your patients."

Scared my arse. I ain't scared. Nothing scares me. I just don't like change, that's all.

"Yeah, all right. Anyway, you gonna ask me?"

"Ask you what?" I know exactly what he's asking me.

"Don't play dumb with me, Dad. Tristan. You always wanna know how he is. Not sure why you can't just call him yourself."

Because he's your best friend, and it's weird. Every time I even hear his voice, my heart starts pounding like some lovestruck creeper. And then the memory of that kiss returns...

Shaking my head, I focus on Jake, who bears an uncanny resemblance to me—brown hair, blue eyes, and a charming smile. Jenny always jokes that after carrying him for 9 months, he finally came out looking like a mini version of me.

"Tell me, how's Tristan?" I cave.

Jake smiles. "I'm about to call him after we've finished talking, but he's good. Still loves his job. I'm about to break it to him that I can't see him this week, because, ya know, Paris!"

"Ditching your best friend for your man, eh?" Now my mind wanders and wants to know if Tristan will be by himself over Christmas. He and Jake used to be glued to the hip, till Tristan dropped out of uni and got himself a job instead.

"Don't say it like that. I worry about Tris enough as it is. He's got a lot on his plate right now."

I'm just about to ask Jake what he's talking about when Lewis appears. "Hey Dax, how's it going?"

"Good, Lewis. Yourself?"

"Yeah, just trying to get this one ready for our trip." He nudges Jake and kisses his cheek. Lewis is a good partner. He loves Jake, and that's all I care about—that my son is happy. Lewis is his person. They've been together for two years now, and I couldn't wish for a better potential son-in-law.

"Jake told me. Lucky you! Maybe you can go visit Grandma and Grandpa. They're spending Christmas in Marseille."

"Yeah maybe. You gonna be okay over Christmas?" Jake's voice takes on that sad tone I don't like. I know he worries about me, too. "We'll come see you when we're back. We still on for a New Year's family night, right?"

"Hell, yeah, we are. Don't worry about me, I'll be fine. Go enjoy yourselves. Lewis, take care of my boy."

"I always do, Dax. Have a good Christmas."

"You too, Lewis. Jake, go get yourself sorted, and text me when you get there, okay?"

"Will do, Dad."

"Love you, son."

"Love you too, Dad."

I hit *End Call*, and pull up my music app, hitting play. The sounds of Michael Bublé fill my kitchen, putting me in a festive mood as I take out my cold toast and slather it in butter. Nothing like buttered cardboard to start your morning.

Chapter Three

"MORNING, DENISE," I GREET the nurse at reception as I sign in. "How is she today?"

"Morning, Tristan. Well, I won't lie, love. She had a bad night. You know how she gets when she doesn't sleep well," she tells me with a sympathetic smile and kind grey eyes that match her hair.

Yeah, I do. It means I won't be staying long this morning. For the past two years, Denise has been one of Mum's dedicated carers at the Willows Dementia Home. At 46, Mum's world was shattered when she received the devastating news that she had the onset of Lewy body dementia. Taking care of her was a daily challenge, as she struggled with confusion and forgetfulness. Despite my best efforts, her hallucinations worsened, leading to alarming calls from neighbours while I was at work, who would find her crying or lost in a daze on the street. She needed more help than I could offer, and I feel guilty about not being good enough for her every day. When she was found walking in and out of traffic near her house, the police were called, and I realised she needed more help. Thankfully, Willows had a place, and she's been here ever since.

"Is she in the day room?"

"Yeah, she's just been given her meds, and Beryl was going to bring her a cup of tea."

I nod as I slip on my visitor's lanyard and make my way to the day room. Spotting Mum by the closed French windows, I make my way over to her. She always loved her garden in our old house. It was beautiful in the spring and summer months. Yellow roses were her favourite. Hanging over her shoulder, her long braid of red hair adds a vibrant splash of colour to her appearance. The green cardigan she's wearing was a labour of love, crafted by her own hands before dementia stole her ability to create. Knitting was her passion. It became increasingly challenging for me to accept that the person I once knew as my mother was fading away before my eyes. Everything we shared just disappeared.

"Hey Mum," I say tenderly, so I don't startle her.

Slowly, she turns her head to look at me, but it's like she's looking right through me. I smile, take off my backpack, and pull up a chair in front of her, taking her hands in mine. "It's me, Tris. Your son." She doesn't reply, but it's fine. I don't need her to. "I brought you some flowers. Harry at the florist told me to say hi. He picked me out the best ones. He knows you only like the big plump roses. And don't worry, I gave them all a squeeze to make sure they're all firm, just the way you taught me. We don't want them wilting too quickly." I find if I ramble to her, it pauses my brain, so I don't think about the fact that I'm basically talking to myself. Looking down, I notice the bow on her slipper has come undone, so I let go of her frail hands and bend to do it back up, so she doesn't trip.

"What are you doing?" she yells, pulling her feet up.

"It's okay, Mum. I'm just tying your bow."

"Get away from me. Who are you?" she spits, her eyes frantic.

I try not to let the sting of her words penetrate me since I know she can't help it. "It's me, Mum. Tristan," I tell her again, but I know it's pointless. She's not with it today.

Beryl walks over with her tea and puts it down on the side table.

"You…" She frantically waves at Beryl. "Help, he's trying to take my shoes. Tell him they're my shoes, he can't have them." Mum has coiled herself up in the chair, her arms wrapped around her legs guarding her shoes. It makes me so sad. This disease is awful.

"Now, now Fern. Tristan is not taking your shoes. Look, he brought you these lovely yellow flowers."

"I don't like flowers. Take them away."

There's no talking to Mum when she's like this. I know it's because she had a bad night. I don't hold it against her. It's not her fault. Doesn't mean it doesn't hurt, though.

"Fern, Tristan is your son. Be nice to him." Bless Beryl for trying.

"He's not my son. I don't have a son. I never wanted kids." She starts pulling at her hair and rocking in the chair. I know it's time for me to go.

I touch Beryl's arm. "It's fine, don't worry. I'll just go leave her flowers and biscuits in her room and I'll come back next week."

"You sure? If you give her a bit of time, her medicine will kick in and she'll calm down." She offers me a sympathetic smile.

"No, it's fine, honestly," I reassure her. "I'm upsetting her today and I don't want that." She nods in understanding, and I pick up the flowers and my backpack and walk out the day room and down the corridor to Mum's room.

Lemon-yellow walls lend a vibrant and airy vibe to the room. On one side, her bed is positioned snugly against the wall, while a chest of drawers occupies the other. The highlight of the room is the expansive window on the far wall, which frames a stunning view of the gardens. I carefully remove the vase of wilted roses from last week from the window seal and discard them. Then, I pour out the old water into the small sink tucked away in the far corner of the room before filling the vase with fresh water. Finally, I arrange the pretty new roses in the vase and take a minute to place them back on the window and arrange them nicely. Then I take out her bourbon biscuits and leave them on her bedside table.

Adorning the wall above her bed, a collection of photographs chronicles the beautiful moments we've shared. Memories that only I remember now. A solitary tear rolls down my face, leaving a trail of sadness in its wake. I hate it. I hate this disease. My mum's been snatched from me. She was all I had. It's really tough when Mum is upset or angry like this, and there's no one else around to understand my pain. It just reminds me of how lonely I am. There's nobody waiting for me at home. It's just me and it really sucks.

As I turn, I glimpse myself in her dresser mirror, my reflection staring back at me. My thick pink hoodie, with its soft fleece lining, is one of my favourites, along with the matching pink joggers. Bright colours have the power to bring happiness to my heart, especially in a world that can often feel dark and gloomy.

Mum and I both share the same flaming red hair, contrasting against our pale skin. Mum's hair is perfectly straight, while mine has a natural, bouncy curl. According to Mum, it's the only thing I got from my dad. Everything else about me is from her. While we both possess a fiery temper, we are also very sensitive at heart. We have slim frames and are five-foot-six, although I used to be overweight at one point. School wasn't fun when you were big and ginger, but I'm not that person anymore. I know he's still inside me and occasionally reminds me he's still there. Like now, when he's telling me we're sad and a tub of *Ben & Jerry's* ice cream will make us feel better.

Nope, not today.

I look at my hat from Trixy still on my head, and it makes me smile. After wiping away my tears and taking a deep breath, I grab my backpack and go to sign out.

I make it to my grey *KIA* without slipping and breaking my neck on the ice. My white *Converse* were probably not the best footwear for today. But I look cute. It's cold as hell; winter is well on its way and I was not made for the cold. I'm just turning the engine on to warm up the car when my phone rings. Pressing *Answer* brings up Jake on *FaceTime*.

"Hey, Jake."

"Hey, Tris. You're in the car. That's not good."

"Yeah, Mum was having a bad day." Jake knew Mum too. We met at university when I thought I wanted to teach English, but uni life wasn't for me. I stuck it out for one year, but I didn't like being away from home, and with the stress of the workload on top of my own mental health and dealing with Mum, it got too much. But Jake and I just clicked, and we've been best friends ever since.

"Damn, I'm sorry to hear that. I was hoping to say hi to her."

"It's fine. Maybe next week will be a good visit. Hey, at least I get to see you this week," I smile.

Jake's face pinches, "Yeah, about that. Um... Lewis's mum invited us to go visit her in Paris. I've been working flat out and really need the break. I'm really sorry, Tris. I know we had plans."

I wave him off, pushing down the tears that threaten to spill from my eyes. "It's fine, Jake. You really do need some time away. You work too hard." I try to keep my voice steady, hoping my disappointment doesn't show.

"Shit, you keep saying you're fine, but I know you're not. Look, I'll cancel the trip. Lewis can go, and we'll stick to our plans."

A traitorous tear slides down my face, and of course, Jake notices it. I swipe it away quickly. "You'll do no such thing, Jake Brooker. I'm honestly fine. I have my own plans for my week off," I lie through my teeth, but Jake, *of course*, sees right through my lying ass.

"No, you don't. You'll lock yourself away in your flat all week, being miserable."

Scowling at him, I sulk. "Well, I'll make some plans then." Poking my tongue out at him, I frown as mean as I can, which is not really mean at all.

He laughs, but it's strained. "I just don't want you to fall back into a bad place. You've worked so hard to get to where you are." His eyes crinkle at the corners with concern.

"I know you worry. I do, too, sometimes, but I'm okay, Jake. I promise. I just get sad when I see Mum."

"I know you do, but me adding to your sadness makes me a shitty friend."

I chuckle. "You're not a shitty friend, you're a great friend. And you also need to look after your own mental health. This trip will do you good."

"I really do need a break. Hey, why don't you go stay at Dad's cabin? It's only a couple of hours away. He won't be there, and at least you'll be squirrelled away in different surroundings."

That's actually not a bad idea. I could be a hermit for a week in a cosy cabin. Some time away to relax and switch off. I've never been to Jake's family cabin, but I've heard him talk about it before. It could be just what I need.

"Yeah alright. You sure your dad won't mind?"

"Nah, he'll be fine. He loves you," Jake chuckles.

Yeah, I love him too. I've had a crush on him since the first day I met him. If I'm being honest, I'm obsessed. I would climb that man like a tree given half the chance.

"I'll send you the address and the code for the key safe on the door." Shit, Jake's still talking while I'm fantasising about his dad. Not cool, Tris. Wind your neck in. Dax is out of bounds. "Just pop into *Tesco* on the way, cos there won't be no food."

"Yeah, okay, I can do that. Thanks, Jake. See, you're not a shitty friend after all," I tease him.

"Yeah, I suppose. I'll let you go so you can get things sorted."

"Okay, cool. Have a safe trip and say hi to Lewis for me. I miss you."

"Miss you too. I'll see you in a week."

Well, my crappy morning just took a turn for the better. And I've just had a great idea to treat myself. I start the car and head to the shopping centre. I've got some gifts to buy.

Chapter Four

A FEW HOURS AWAY my arse! I've been driving for nearly four sodding hours. We won't count the snack breaks because they're mandatory. Everybody knows a *Greggs'* steak bake, and *McDonald's* chips are a staple at the services.

Following Jake's directions, I find myself driving closer to the breathtaking landscape of Snowdonia. Apparently, Dax's parents had plans to purchase him a luxurious beach house in the south of France for his twenty-first birthday. However, he had other ideas in mind, like wanting a fixer-upper closer to home. So, they bought him a cabin in Wales. According to Jake, it's a tradition for him and his dad to spend their summers there, bonding while they repair and improve the place. He said they used to go hiking, and then camp out under the stars. It sounds wonderful.

There are moments when I ponder about my father's character, and whether I have any similarities to him. What would life have been like if he were around. It was always just me and Mum.

When I asked her about my dad, she gave a vague response, mentioning that he wasn't ready for commitment. She was determined to give me the best life she could, even though she was on her own.

We were always poor, and I had to wait to get the things my friends had, all the new toys that came out or the latest trend in fashion and by the time Mum had saved for it, it was no longer popular. Even with our tight food budget, she found a way to prepare yummy meals for us. Working at a bakery close by, she would bring home the day's leftovers, ensuring that our plates were always full. Unfortunately, this also contributed to my weight gain during my teenage years. Despite everything, she always gave her best and made me her top priority. There was never a shortage of love in our house.

Mum was my best friend till I met Jake. Her warm words of encouragement never failed to lift my spirits. The dementia has taken away so much, including the memories of the little things that made her who she was. I miss her even though she's still here.

Swiping away the stray tears of my memories so I don't crash the car, I remind myself that we never know what tomorrow may bring, so live in the moment. I'm determined to enjoy this cabin break.

It feels like I've been driving on the A5 for half my life when some knobhead cuts me off. "Watch out, you bloody idiot!" Slamming on the breaks, as I try to regain my composure. Jesus, I swear people are getting worse at driving, not better. Who cuts someone up on an A-road? Mr *Audi* Twat Waffle, that's who.

On the side of the road, a big red spray-painted sign for a Christmas market catches my eye. Deciding I could really use a break to stretch my legs, I take the next left and follow the signs. I end up in a car park bustling with activity. Luckily, I'm able to snag an empty bay. There's so much excitement all around this time of year. It makes me smile as a cute couple walks past, hand in hand, wearing matching red bobble hats.

There's a festive sparkle in the air as anticipation builds and people rush to the shops to stock up on delicious Christmas food and goodies ready for the big day.

Acting on Jake's advice, I made a detour to Tesco's on my way here, loading up my car with a *tempting* array of snacks and goodies to last me the entire week. It's a good thing it's cold out—my stuff will stay cool in the car while I have a quick mooch around the market.

Getting out of the car with Trixy's hat snugly on my head, I hastily zip up my cosy, furry blue coat and slide my hands into my gloves. I'm glad I dressed warmly today with my blue cargo pants and black *Buffalos*. It's freezing out here. Still no snow, but looking upwards, the sky is just pure white, a sure sign that it's on the way. I take extra care as I walk because the ice on the ground makes it slippery. No broken bones here, thank you.

First off, I need a hot chocolate, extra creamy. My nose hunts down the food truck selling the warm, chocolaty goodness.

"You want marshmallows?" asks the older lady currently making my drink.

"It's a crime not to have them." I offer her a broad smile.

"My thoughts exactly. Here you go, love," she sing-songs.

"Thank you. Have a good day."

With my new drink in hand, I sip it while strolling through the busy market. The stalls are all decked out with lights and garlands. A mixture of cinnamon and vanilla invades my senses. All the deliciously sweet treats smell amazing.

My Christmases used to be a time spent with Mum, but since she went into the nursing home, it's just been me. Even though Mum's memories of Christmas may fade, I refuse to let the festive spirit wane. So, I walk around the market soaking in the sights and smells while I load up on my festive cheer.

Walking past a local cheese stall reminds me of the last couple of Christmases when Jake and Lewis would come over in the evenings, and we would indulge in a feast of cheese and crackers while watching Christmas films until we fell into a food coma. We would improvise a camp on the living room floor using cushions and duvets, as I only had a tiny, one-bedroom flat. A wave of sadness tries to pull me down as I realise I won't get to experience that this year. I stop and take a deep, calming breath. Nope, bugger off, melancholy. I'm going to have my own little Christmas in a cabin in the Welsh forest. If only I had someone to spend it with, but hopefully one day, I'll meet that special someone. Who knows, right?

As if on cue, whenever I think of my future with a possible partner, the image of Jake's dad pops into my head and my lips tingle with the ghost sensation of that one kiss. The kiss to end all kisses. Ugh, stop it, Tris! No reason to go wishing for things that aren't going to come true, anyway.

With a demonstrative pep in my step and more pretty stalls to look at, I carry on round the market. I can't resist picking up some vibrant baubles; my lack of self-control and the joy of spending money get the best of me. It's not until I reach the last stall where I've just bought a bright red bauble that says '*Balls Deep*' that it dawns on me—I have nothing to hang the baubles on. As far as I know from the stories Jake has told me, Dax only goes to the cabin in the spring and summer months. So, I doubt he has anything there that's Christmas-y. Good going, Tris. No tree, just a bag full of balls. With a shrug, I decide to just save them for next year.

On my way back to the car, I must have taken a detour through the market, because in front of me is the stall I need.

Sixty quid later, and I'm the owner of a real tree. I feel robbed! The tree in question is just chilling on the roof of my car. No regard for how much the bugger just cost me. Mr Spruce is tied down with some rope the tree guy gave me. Thank God the satnav says I've only got 30 minutes left. My excitement at finally getting there is bubbling. I crank up the volume on the car stereo, the sound of Tony Bennett singing '*Winter Wonderland*' blasting my ears as I drive the last few miles.

Half an hour later, I turn down the music *so I can see better*. I'm currently driving up a steep road, and I can feel the tyres sliding. Just up ahead, I see a quaint brown cabin nestled among the trees. With no other buildings around, I'm guessing this must be it. Pulling up outside, I shut off the engine and check the message Jake sent with all the details.

The sign next to the front door is visible from the car window.

Big Bear Cabin.

Looks like I'm here. I get out of the car and take in my surroundings with a little spin. Towering trees surround the cabin, their branches stretching towards the sky like they are reaching for something I can't see. Some of them still cling to their last remaining brown leaves. It's quiet here and a little eerie. The animals in the forest are probably all snuggled up for winter hibernation. The only sign of life here is me.

I shiver in the bitter cold as I take in the large, dark wood cabin. It's much bigger than I was expecting. Since I kind of had a small shed in mind, this is a mansion in my book. It looks like Dax has taken good care of the place, although it's clear that no one has been here recently with all the scattered leaves that have built up. Jake's comment about his dad's preference for summer visits suddenly makes sense. But *I'm* here now to love on this place and keep it company.

On the left-hand side of the porch, a pile of chopped wood fills a storage box. The box is sitting under a large window. Next to it, a broom and shovel are mounted on the front wall of the cabin. A large red shed is situated just off to the side of the building. Moving closer to the front steps, looking over to my right, there's a wooden bench under the next window that invites you to sit and enjoy the views of the Welsh countryside. On the backrest, I can just make out the names Dax and Jake, not very skilfully carved, but it's cute all the same.

Holding onto the rail as I walk up the four timber steps, my feet crunch frost-covered leaves. Just as Jake said, there is a small brown box with a cute little door sitting next to the large wooden front door. A keypad is revealed when I pull it open, and I punch in the code Jake sent me. Taking the cold metal key in my hand, I close the box and insert it into the lock.

Pushing the door open, I'm instantly hit with a musty smell, but it's not unpleasant. There's something comforting about the mix of dust, wood, and a hint of spice as I step inside and stamp my feet on the mat. Looking around near the door for a light switch, I'm greeted by an imposing axe on the wall. I hope I don't need to use that to fight off a yeti!

The room bursts into life, pleasantly surprising me, and I survey the space, my gaze bouncing around. There are high ceilings, at least twelve feet tall, and wood beams frame the building. The left side of the cabin is open plan, with the living room and kitchen areas merged. It's bright and airy, with large windows showcasing the stunning views. I can already imagine how cosy the place will feel once I get the fire going. If I'd known how great this place was, I would have brought more decorations.

Two rustic-looking chandeliers hang from the beams. One in front of the brick fireplace that climbs the wall to the roof, and another in front of me by the door. The tan sofa positioned in front of the fireplace has my name on it. I can't wait to snuggle up on it.

My gaze wanders around the room, to the kitchen. It's a decent size that blends beautifully with the cabin's dark wood décor. A table and two chairs sit in the middle, a cute red-and-white tablecloth on top.

All around the dark wooden floor, large cream rugs fill the space. To my right are two doors. I open the door closest to me, and a quick look inside reveals a bathroom with a large claw-foot bath and an overhead shower. *Yes, please*, to a long soak in there tonight, I think.

Closing the door, I make my way to the second one, pushing it open to reveal the only bedroom. Strange that there's only one room in here.

This room is stunning, though. A king-size bed sits proudly in the middle of the room, a navy cover and cream blanket draped across the end. It, too, is surrounded by a large rug that stretches across most of the floor.

As I explore the room, my eyes gravitate towards the dark, fitted wardrobe on the left-hand side. Curiosity gets the better of me, and I slide open one door. Yes, they are on fancy runners. The sight that greets me is a treasure trove of clothes belonging to Dax, I assume. I can't resist the urge to run my hand along the row of cardigans, savouring the feel of the soft wool against my face as I inhale deeply. The faint smell of cologne lingers on the blue cardigan I'm currently smushing my face into. Dax must have worn it before hanging it back up. It's a musky scent with subtle notes of teakwood. It's absolutely heavenly.

There's nothing like a man in a cardi to get my pulse peaking and my cock a-leaking!

I make my way over to the double window, taking in the heavy, floor-length navy curtains. Looking outside to a picturesque scene of the sprawling forest and the road I had recently driven up, the peaceful beauty of the world unfolds before me, soothing my mind.

The leaves and ground are adorned with a faint frost, sparkling like tiny diamonds, a promise of the snow to come, hiding it all until spring. Everything is tranquil and beautiful. When a shiver runs through me, I'm reminded that I need to unpack the car and get some heat going in this place. As stunning as the cold looks right now, I have a feeling it gets bloody crisp in here at night.

I get to work starting a fire in the big-ass fireplace, so I don't freeze to death. No, thank you. The cold and I are not besties.

Conveniently—and luckily—everything I need is nearby. Logs, kindling, and matches are all neatly piled in a basket next to the hearth, likely left by Dax precisely for this reason. While I've never made a fire before, I'm going to give it my best shot.

After assembling the logs into a cone shape, I ignite a small piece of kindling and carefully place it at the centre, ensuring it continues to burn. Lots of late-night *TikTok* reels have come in handy! I knew there was a reason for me staying up late, doom-scrolling my phone every night. Just call me Bear Grylls.

Dax has clearly put a lot of effort into renovating this cabin, and I'm glad I decided to come here. Now that the fire is blazing, the cabin emanates a warm, homely atmosphere. I love how the walls are adorned with framed pictures of him and Jake. He really is a great dad to my best friend.

For a moment, I miss Mum again. I can't help it. She would have loved it here. I can envision her baking in the kitchen all day, then sitting by the fire, knitting in the evenings. It hurts my heart so much that she won't get to experience these things in life anymore, and to top it off, she doesn't even remember the things she did accomplish. But I'm reassured knowing she's well looked after in Willows. I linger in my sadness for a few more moments, but I know I need to pull up my big boy pants, or lack thereof because commando is how I roll. Standing, I take a deep breath and get back on track for my week here.

I bring in my shopping and store it all away. The kitchen provides everything you could need in a cabin: a fridge, freezer, a large double oven, and a dishwasher. Earlier I found a laundry room and the door to a pantry that was still well-stocked with dry foods. My whole flat would fit in the living room of this place. I can't wait to make this cabin smell amazing with all the Christmas cooking I plan to do. I'm only a bit sad that it will only be me eating it all. But It's fine. *I'm fine.*

Once I'm finished in the kitchen, I make my way to the bedroom to unpack, moving over some of Dax's clothes in the wardrobe to put mine in their place. Looking at the garments I brought with me, it's clear they were not meant for the forest. But seeing as it's just me here this week, I still wanted to feel sexy. Basically, crop tops, shorts, and a couple of barely there skirts.

Next, I place my favourite dildo in the bedside drawer alongside Dax's knick-knacks. It's an eight-inch replica, mimicking the real deal, complete with prominent testicles that make a satisfying sound against my arse when I thrust into my hole. While it may not match the feel of a real dick in my arse, I have no complaints! I'm not going to be celibate just because I'm in the middle of nowhere. I'm a sexual person! Actually, I might even jerk off in front of the fire tonight and pretend it's Dax's hand.

I slip on my vibrant-red boots Jeb found for me in a charity shop and wrap myself up in my coat before heading outside to the car to bring in the tree. The approaching night casts a shadow over the surroundings, transforming them into a somewhat ominous sight. The serene brightness of the day is fading, replaced by a calm yet mysterious darkness. Where's a burly lumberjack when you need 'im?

With a grunt, I heave the tree off the back of the car roof, and it thuds onto the floor. Pine needles scatter as I struggle to drag its thick trunk towards the steps. My feet slide from under me and end up landing on my butt. "*OOF.* That's gonna hurt later, and I didn't even get pounded," I say to the quiet forest. "Whose brilliant idea was it to get a tree?" I mumble. "Oh, yeah, mine."

Despite my wet and uncomfortable rear end, I persevere, dusting myself off, and hauling the beast into the cabin. For now, it can temporarily stand in the corner between the window and the fireplace. That's a tomorrow problem.

With pine needles digging into me and damp clothes, I head to the bedroom to swap into comfy green shorts that perfectly complement my ginger curls. I pair them with my favourite pink crop top, adorned with a lollipop graphic that cheekily says, '*Suck it.*' Ready to satisfy my hunger, I make my way to the kitchen, hit *Play* on a playlist on my phone, and sway my hips to Shakin Stevens' '*Merry Christmas Everyone.*'

Chapter Five

Fuck. That was a bloody hard workout. Throwing my keys on my kitchen side, I go to grab cold water from the fridge. Who thought it would be a good idea to try to compete with the college kids in the gym this morning?

This dickhead.

Who's paying for it now?

This dickhead.

I'm no spring chicken and doing a hundred pull-ups followed by an eight-minute sprint has me needing a hot shower and some ibuprofen. Who was I even trying to impress?

The young twenty-something guys today just thought I was some kind of idiot, nearly dropping a dumbbell on my foot, trying to look like I knew what I was doing. It's not like I have a partner to look good for, but I try my best to keep in shape when I can. I don't even have another date lined up for next week yet. I doubt I'll even get one with it being the week before Christmas. What a sad sack of shit I am, probably spending the holiday on my own with just my hand for comfort. My mind wanders to a certain guy that I have no business letting one thought about enter my mind. I try to block out the night that always seems to work its way into my memories, but it's no good.

"Come on, Dad. Come meet my friends and have a drink. It's my birthday," Jake asked me that day on the phone. Turning twenty-one, he decided against a traditional family celebration and instead organised a night out at the local gay bar with his college friends. He hardly ever wanted me to tag along, maybe because he didn't want me to mess up his cool image, but I treasured any time I got to be with him, so I jumped at the chance.

Shaking my head to erase the thoughts before they get any further, I toss my empty water bottle into the recycling and make my way upstairs. With each step, I can already feel the relief of shedding my damp gym clothes, and stepping into the soothing spray of my ensuite shower is just what my body needs to unwind.

Once I'm clean, I know I should get out, but of course, the temptation of jacking off is too much. My dick is fully onboard. As I tug on my semi-hard cock, my thumb grazes over the textured bumps lining the top of my shaft. Six of them, which I had specifically added for my partner's pleasure four years ago. Pearling. I'd seen it in a porno and was intrigued. With some more research, I knew it was something I wanted to have done.

Firmly planting my other hand on the shower wall, I shut my eyes tightly and attempt to divert my thoughts away from *him*. Yet, no matter how forcefully I try, his face keeps appearing, and I have no choice but to surrender to the overwhelming memories of that night.

Stepping through the bar's front door, the boisterous sound of cheers echoed through the air, setting the energetic tone of the place. It was then that I noticed a cute guy walking towards me, his blue eyes sparkling like raindrops, and a flirtatious smile on his lips. His lean body was clad in shiny silver shorts, and a baby blue see-through mess top, his perky pink nipples on display. Fiery red curls bounced on his head.

With no words shared, he brazenly slid his arms around my neck and pulled my head down into a kiss. Despite my initial hesitation, his tongue danced across my lips, igniting a fire within me, and my arms eagerly embraced him, pulling him closer as I willingly surrendered myself to him. The sweet taste of the alcohol blended with his natural flavour created a sensation that was intoxicating. His warm breath coasted over me. As the kiss deepened, our heads turned to draw closer, both of us lost in a moment, forgetting our surroundings, as we consumed each other, strangers that seemed to fit together instinctively.

My hand ventured down his back, searching for something to hold on to, until it discovered his enticing ass cheek, perfectly moulded to fit in my grasp, securing him against my growing cock. My other hand lovingly caressed his face.

His whimper lingers in my mind, trapped in a never-ending loop, tormenting me.

My hand moves with increased speed and force, as I recall the sensation of him, aching for the opportunity to turn back time and experience it all once more. It's wrong, but I'm too far gone to stop. If I try hard enough, I swear I can still taste him. My lips tingled with the memory of his, so plump and smooth, pressing against mine with a firmness that I couldn't forget.

With my eyes shut tight, the feel of warm water against my skin intensifies the pleasure I felt from one hand jacking my dick while the other gently tugs on my balls. What I wouldn't give to kiss him again, to feel his lithe body in my hands, to know what it would feel like to pump my load into his tight little hole…

Fuck.

Waves of excitement surge through my body, starting from the base of my spine and coursing through every inch of me. My stomach tightens, and a rush of pleasure cascades over me as his name escapes my lips in a passionate cry.

Tristan.

There's nothing quite like the sound of a cold beer cracking open. A day dedicated to chilling out and doing absolutely nothing. Drinking and watching sports. Sitting on my brown leather sofa, I barely have time to lift the bottle to my lips before my phone interrupts with a loud ring. Picking it up, my heart skips a beat at the sight of Tristan's name on the screen, but in the next moment, a wave of worry washes over me as I realise he's never called me before. The only reason I have his number is because I convinced Jake that I might need it in case of an emergency. After much persuasion, he finally agreed to add it to my contacts. I've lost count of how many times I've stared at the number, desperately hoping it would ring, just so I could hear Tristan's voice. It's bordering on stalker-ish.

"Hello?" I ask hesitantly.

"OH MY GOD, DAX! HELP, WATER, EVERYWHERE..." A shrill, panicked voice sounds from the other end.

"What? What do you mean, water?"

"Water... in the bathroom. Oh, God, what do I do? I didn't know what to do, Dax. I called you. Shit. Towels. I need towels."

"Tristan!" I shout loud enough for me to break through his panic.

"What?" he screeches, the panic lingering in his voice.

Using my soothing teacher's voice, even though my own nerves are frayed, I gently instruct, "First, take a deep breath for me." I hear him inhaling, his breathing clipped. "Okay, let's start from the beginning. Where are you now and what's happening?"

"I'm currently at your cabin. Jake was supposed to spend this week with me, but he ended up going to Paris with Lewis. So, he suggested I stay here so I could unwind and avoid feeling miserable in my apartment. I arrived yesterday. I was just prepping food when I heard a loud gushing noise. Water is leaking from under the bathroom sink, and I called you because I didn't know what else to do."

The moment I hear the building anxiety in his voice, it stirs something inside me. He reached out to me, and that realisation settles deep within me. I am the one he needs. It doesn't matter that he had no one else to call, or that he was in my cabin; I'm intentionally disregarding those details and instead choosing to concentrate on the significance of him *needing me*. Pathetic, I know, but I never said I was a smart man.

"Okay, don't worry. You did the right thing calling me."

"Yeah?" he breathes into the phone. *Yes,* my inner protector growls. *Always call me!*

"Of course. Let's start with the basics. Head over to the kitchen sink. Look inside the cupboard, and you'll find a tap with a red cover, should be right at the back."

As he walks across my cabin floor, I can hear the soft pad of his feet. Is he wearing socks? Or is he barefoot? Who the fuck cares, Dax? Focus!

"Okay, I see it," he pants.

"Good, now turn the red stopcock counterclockwise and that will shut off the water to the cabin. You'll be without it for a few hours while I drive to you, but at least it should have stopped the water in the bathroom."

"Wait, you're coming here?" Surprise is evident in his voice.

I hear a bang down the phone as he slams the cupboard door closed. His voice carries a subtle undertone that I can't quite decipher—is it relief, shock, or maybe a small sign he doesn't want me at the cabin? No, that's ridiculous. He definitely wants me there. I need to fix the problem because that's what I am here: *a problem fixer,* not a guy who pines for his son's best friend.

Jesus, brain, get a grip. It's not happening, *nothing* is happening here. There is not a Tristan for you in this lifetime.

You drive.

You fix.

You leave.

"Yeah, I'll need to check for any burst pipes; otherwise, there's a risk of flooding in the cabin, and you won't have any water during your stay."

"Oh right, yeah, good plan. Okay, so... I'll go clean up the water and wait for you to come? I mean arrive."

A smile breaks out on my face at his misuse of words. *Come.* Yeah, I'd like to come all over... for fuck's sake, Dax. I catch myself and shake off the thought.

"I'll be there in a few hours. And Tris?"

"Yeah," he says in a breathy voice that goes straight to my balls. *Tris...* Since when do I shorten his name? It slipped out my mouth like it belonged there. "Don't worry, I'll get it sorted."

"You're my hero," he chuckles.

Fuck, the sound of his happiness is almost painful. Was he really going to spend all week locked up in my cabin by himself? This hits a nerve. He should be looked after by a loving partner, enjoying the fun of Christmas, not hauled up in the middle of nowhere alone. But who was I kidding? I was gonna hide in my house all week doing the same thing.

I need to see Tristan for myself, just to make sure that he's okay. That's all this feeling is. Concern.

After ending the call, I turn off the TV and double-check that the back door is securely locked. The shed at the cabin already holds all the tools I'll need. My clothes are already there too, so I don't have to bring anything. However, I do take the blue blanket from the back of my couch. If it's a hero he wants, it's a hero he'll get. I crank up the heat in the car and switch the radio station to *Heart.* '*All I Want for Christmas'* blares through the speakers. I sing along enthusiastically as I drive towards the cabin, eager to see Tristan. Maybe a little too eagerly, but I won't dwell on that now.

Chapter Six

GOD, I'M EXCITED BUT nervous that Dax is coming here. *The Dax of my dreams.* The one who I kissed on Jake's birthday three years ago. The one who I try to catch on FaceTime when I'm over at Jake's flat. I've been crushing hard on the guy for years, pictured in my fantasies what being with him would look like. How would it feel to be with him? Would it be as good as in my imagination? I want that man so badly. It's not like I can just casually turn up at Dax's house and say, 'I'm horny. Wanna fuck?'

I think back to the first night we met at Jake's twenty-first. We'd all been drinking and playing Truth or Dare. I took the dare.

"I got a good one," Jake declared, rubbing his hands together. "You have to kiss the next guy who walks through the door."

"Lame. What if the guy is old?" I'd complained.

"Tough tits! You took the dare. You have no choice," John, one of Jake's uni buddies, hit back.

"Fine," I grumbled, knocking back my shot. All the guys were whooping and hollering as I got up and made my way closer to the door to await my fate. As the door opened, I held my breath. In walked a sexy DILF wearing a black polo-neck jumper, dark grey slacks, and fancy-looking Italian shoes. His brown hair was a touch messy and had the finest sprinkling of grey in the sideburns. The chocolate brown of his eyes made my butthole flutter as he gave me the once over. He took off his glasses, sliding them into his pants pocket.

Yes, the gods were in my favour. I just hoped he didn't get me arrested for pouncing on him because there was no way in hell I was gonna pass up a kiss with this fine wine. I literally threw myself at him before he had the chance to turn me away.

Boy, could this guy kiss. My toes curled as I wrapped myself around him. Firm lips opened at the slightest touch of my tongue. Everything around me faded away as I gobbled him up. It was a proper 'Meet Cute,' just like in films.

When we eventually parted so we could catch our breath, Jake was standing next to us, laughing.

"Hey, Dad. I see you've met Tristan!"

Yeah, I'd kissed my best friend's dad. What a cliché, if it wasn't for the fact our kiss had been one for the books.

I adjust myself in my shorts as I make my way past the sofa just as the front door swings open, a cold gust of wind swirling around the image of my dreams in a fucking knitted cardigan and a blue blanket around his shoulders like... a cape. *Dax.*

Standing in the doorway, he paints a stunning picture, with the newly started flurries as a natural backdrop. The scent of pine, fresh air, and the spice I picked up on the first day here that I now recognise as Dax. His cologne must be made of pheromones because it's calling to me like a cold drink on a hot day. Be still my pulsing balls!

Thank God, I went for my loose-fitting baby-pink shorts and white Christmas crop top that says 'HO, HO, HOE,' because Dax is looking all kinds of flustered right now. It's exactly the effect I wanted to achieve... when I tried on five different outfits while waiting for him to get here.

I take in the man I've had many—and I mean *many*—orgasms over. His knitted cardi buttoned up to his sternum, clinging to his well-built frame, underneath it a white T-shirt, and blue jeans that fit him like a glove. I'm struggling so badly to hold back the whimper that wants to burst free from my body.

"You're here," I pant. He must have driven at the speed of light; it's only been a few hours since I called him.

"Hey, Tristan. Sorry for barging in, but it's starting to blow up a storm out there. I used my key. I hope that's okay?"

Kind and considerate. Noted. "It's your place, so you don't need to ask to come in," I smile. In a sexy way, I hope, and not in an '*I wanna make sweet love to you all night*' kind of stare. "Is... is that cape for me?" I squeak and there goes sexy right out the window, needy taking its place instead.

Dax huffs and removes the blanket from around his shoulders, folding it up. "Yeah," he mumbles. "Stupid idea. I thought it would be cute."

"You are! I mean, it is. Cute," I rush out. "Thank you. No one has ever been my hero before." My fists clench as I try to stop my core memory of just pouncing on him from taking over.

The frown on his face makes me wonder if I've upset him by saying that. Or maybe it's pity? Well, this is awkward. I've made him feel uncomfortable in his own cabin.

"So, umm... the bathroom?" he says, rubbing the back of his neck.

"Oh, yes." Rushing over to the bathroom door, I push it open while Dax closes the front door, his boots thudding on the mat. "I tried to mop up the water the best I could. I left a few towels down in case any more water decided to blast out. It hit me in the face like a pubescent boy when I opened the door earlier."

A slight smile tugs at one corner of his mouth. "Let me take a look, then I'll go grab my tools from the shed and see if I can't fix this."

I shift in the doorway to let Dax pass, feeling the closeness as his chest grazes mine. "Okay, I'll leave you to it then. I'll go do... *something* in the kitchen." I say. "Just shout if you need me to do anything."

Dax acknowledges with a nod and then promptly falls to his knees in front of the cupboard while I cautiously step back. While examining the pipes, he leans in and his shirt and cardi slide up, exposing his sun-kissed lower back. The jeans cling tightly to his butt, offering a subtle view of his crack. It's all but waving at me with its little red flag. *Lick me.*

The whimper I had been suppressing finally breaks free, joined by the unmistakable thump of Dax's head colliding with the cupboard. Oops. It's time to make a quick retreat before I do any more damage to him.

I'm bored in the kitchen, twiddling my thumbs. While I waited for Dax to arrive, I finished preparing the dinner. The delightful scent of a chicken casserole fills the kitchen as it simmers on low in the oven. The chocolate chip cookies, still warm from the oven, beckon me from the tray. I resist the temptation to pick one up, knowing that they need more time to cool and set in the middle. So, I'm left with nothing to do.

Dax is banging about in the bathroom. I dare not go back in there, as I'm likely to slide my hand down his jeans and fondle his cheeks. Self-control has never been my strong suit, to be honest.

Without a television in this cabin, finding entertainment has been a challenge for the past twenty-four hours; there's only so much time I can spend jacking off before I make my dick red and raw.

I notice my sad Christmas tree, still leaning against the cabin wall. Walking over to where it's standing, all six feet of it, I gently graze my fingertips along the sharp, prickly needles, applying pressure to a pine branch to unleash its fragrance as I lean in to take a deep sniff.

"You need a stand and a water bucket for that before it dies," a deep voice washes over me.

I turn my head so quickly that I almost give myself whiplash. Dax is a hair's breadth away from me. His cardigan is long gone, and he's wearing just the white T-shirt that's now covered in brown smears. His tanned arms are devoid of any tattoos, just a layer of light brown hair.

"*What*?" comes out in a shaky breath. Still as good-looking as I remember. The addition of a few more fine lines enhances his kind, clean-shaven, handsome face.

Gesturing to the tree, he continues, "It's warm in here with the fire going, so it's drying out the tree. It needs a stand or a bucket. If you don't water it soon, you'll be decorating sticks." The smile on his face makes me want to reach out and touch it, the tips of my fingers tingling.

"Oh." It suddenly occurs to me I didn't pick up anything like that when I bought the tree. I have a strong inclination to go find the tree guy on my way home and confront him with some prickly pine needles for selling me an incomplete tree.

"Don't worry," Dax chuckles. "Once I've sorted out the pipe, I can sort something." My hero saves the day again. *Fucking swoon.*

With Dax so close to me, my words seem to have vanished, leaving me only able to nod my head and nervously lick my lips. I can't help but notice that Dax attentively follows every movement of my tongue.

His brown eyes flick up to me, knowing he's been caught. Taking a step back, he croaks, "Can you, er... do me a favour and boil the kettle? The pipe outside has frozen. That's the cause of the water. It had nowhere to go but up out of the sink. I just need to defrost and cover it so it doesn't happen again."

"Hum? What?" I ask, too busy watching Dax's lips move as he's talking to me, my brain switching off.

"The kettle? Can you boil it for me while I go take a look outside?" He throws me a puzzled frown.

Dropping the branch I was still holding clears my brain fog. "Yeah, course. I'll do that now." Turning to avoid any more stupidness on my part, I make my way to the kitchen, hearing the door close behind me.

Once the kettle boils, I wait a few minutes, straining my ears for any sign of Dax, but all I hear is the crackling of the fire. Deciding to pull my finger out my arse, I try to be of any help, seeing as it was me that dragged him all the way here in the first place. I slip on my red boots by the front door, put on my puffy coat, and grab the kettle.

The moment I open the door, a rush of frigid wind and delicate snowflakes chill my legs to the bone. The weather is far from ideal for wearing shorts, but I have no other option since the only trousers I have were the ones I arrived in. They're still waiting to be washed, along with the wet towels from today. Guess I'm wearing shorts in the snow.

I hear noise coming from the left, my curiosity leading me to discover Dax crouched in front of the outside pipe, diligently sweeping away fallen leaves from the area with gloved hands.

"Hey!" I call out against the wind.

Dax stands and turns to me, the same frown from earlier on his face. His cheeks are now rosy from the cold, his hair blowing around from the wind that has picked up. "What the hell are you doing out here with nothing on? Are you trying to make yourself sick?" His tone is harsh and hits me at my core. I go from one hundred to zero in a split second, wanting to recoil in on myself. The smile on my face is long gone, and I'm left feeling the loss of it.

Looking down at my slim legs, a fine coating of ginger hair leads down into my boots, and I swear my skin is starting to turn blue. Shifting my gaze over to another set of black boots that don't belong to me, my eyes slowly trail up jean-covered legs to a thick brown winter coat, finally meeting the concerned eyes of the man acting like a dad. Was I just being scolded as a child or an incompetent adult? Jake's lucky to have a dad who gives a shit about people, but being yelled at takes me to a dark place. One I don't want to revisit right now.

"Sorry, I didn't think," I murmur quietly. "I just wanted to bring you out the kettle." Shoving the hot water at him, I turn and make my way back inside. I'm feeling all kinds of stupid, and butt hurt now as I hang up my coat on the pegs near the door. Placing my damp red boots on the floor underneath, I shake off the feeling of embarrassment at being told off.

If I want to wear next to no clothes, I will. It's taken me a long time to feel comfortable in my body and to wear the clothes I feel most like me in. Granted, wearing them in nearly freezing temperatures was probably not one of my better calls, but that's beside the point. It was my call to make. All I wanted to do was help. They say no good deed goes unpunished.

After I've eaten two of my cookies, I feel a bit better, but I don't want to fall into the trap of eating too many. Emotional eating is not my friend. So, I transfer the rest to a plate and wrap them up, then check on my casserole and thicken it up with some gravy granules, giving it all a stir and returning it to the oven.

To keep myself busy till Dax comes back in, I lay the table for us both. Mum would be mad if I sent him home on an empty stomach. Not that she would ever know, but I would. She didn't raise me like that. *'We share what we have, even if it isn't much,'* she used to say.

I smile at the memory as I throw a few more logs on the fire, so it's nice and warm for when Dax comes back in. Because, unlike him, I'm not an arsehole. I need him to know I might not have the best outside dress choices, but I can look after myself and his cabin.

Chapter Seven

SHIT. I CURSE MYSELF as I kick the side of the cabin after hearing the door slam. I fucked up and hurt Tristan's feelings. I could see it in the look on his face. It was like I'd taken a dagger to his heart. Sad blue eyes met mine, and I instantly regretted my words. I didn't mean any harm, but seeing him out here in the freezing cold in the shortest fucking shorts known to man, with his bare legs out, just sent my protectiveness into overdrive.

His slim legs, which I couldn't seem to take my eyes off, had been turning a light shade of blue from the cold. What I wanted to do was pick him up and carry him back inside, place him by the fire, and wrap him up in... well, me. But instead, I made him feel bad. I shouldn't have gone all dad mode on him. He's a twenty-four-year-old man and I have no business telling him what he can and can't wear. Fucking hell's bells. He calls me here to help him and all I do is berate him.

I put Tristan to the back of my mind for the time being, as I need to focus on fixing the pipe. On the drive here, the radio forecast that heavy snow is on the way. The light flurrying that started about an hour ago is already getting heavier, sticking to my coat, and the cold wind is starting to sting my face. If I want to get home tonight, I need to get a move on.

As I pour the hot water onto the metal pipe, wisps of steam immediately begin to rise and dance in the air. I have only been waiting for a few minutes when I hear the familiar sound of water rushing through the pipe again. This time, the fix is straightforward and quick. As I approach the porch, I place the kettle down before making my way to the shed to retrieve the rest of the items needed to complete the job.

The shed is wired with electricity and stands at the same height as the cabin. The choice of red paint was a nod to Jake's childhood fascination with toy fire engines. It appears I share a liking for the colour red as well.

After flipping the light switch, I survey the inside. Neatly stacked piles of wood flank each side of the doorway, waiting to be split and brought onto the porch. The smell of damp, musty wood fills the space, but it differs from what I'm used to. In the summer, I'm accustomed to the dry wood that reminds me of crackling campfires and the aroma of toasted marshmallows and hot dogs.

Originally, I built it as storage for all Jake's toys. He was only knee-high to a grasshopper when I finally started to work on renovating the cabin. It was run-down and needed lots of work, but it was structurally sound. We spent every summer out here, and even Jenny used to come when Jake was still a toddler, but as he got older, it was just me and him. When he was younger, we shared a room, each of us having a single bed, but once Jake got older, he wanted his own space, so the sofa became my bed, unless we were out camping.

Now there are no longer paddle boards and camping gear on the back shelf. Nor fishing rods and bikes mounted on the wall. Saws and tools are now in their place, and all my summer gear is neatly packed away.

As Jake grew up and became focused on uni, he would only make it out here for a few weeks in the summer holidays. It's been a good few years since he's been here. My little boy is, after all, a grown man now. But some things are of too sentimental value to get rid of, like the mud painting Jake did when he was five. It still hangs on the shed wall, his grubby handprints still visible on the canvas.

In the far corner, I have a big box of random things that always seem to come in handy when I least expect it. We used to call it the crap box. You know that box you put absolutely everything in because '*one day you might need it*?' I grab one of Jake's old pool noodles and a standing knife, then cut it to the length I need. With the blue noodle in hand, I make my way outside along with some duct tape and secure the foam to the pipe to stop it from freezing up again.

Loading up the wheelbarrow, I top up the wood stores on the porch. Then I find a bucket big enough to fit the Christmas tree in. The bricks I was saving to make an herb garden in the spring will come in handy. By adding weights to the big plant pot, they can stabilise the tree and prevent it from toppling over. I rummage through the boxes and finally find the string of lights that I normally hang around the porch during the summer. After all, what's a tree without twinkling lights?

Despite my best efforts to deny it, I know very well that I'm procrastinating, hesitating to face Tristan inside. But now I'm running out of things to do. With the snow showing no signs of letting up, I gather my courage to go inside, ready to face Tristan, hoping to be forgiven so I can head home.

Pushing the front door open, I'm greeted not only by the delicious smell of food, but Tristan with his back to me in those bloody shorts and crop top. I nearly swallow my tongue, watching him dish up two steaming bowls. My stomach growls and my mouth waters, but not for the food. My glasses steam up from being outside in the cold and then walking into the warmth of the cabin. Everything goes blurry as I take them off to clean them with the hem of my jacket so I can see again. Short-sighted, that's what the opticians told me five years ago. Nothing like a pair of glasses to make me feel like an old man. The first pair I bought made Jake laugh; he described them as grandad glasses because of their gold-rimmed frames and oversized lenses. Of course, he insisted I go back with him to buy some hip ones, to avoid the kids at school taking the piss out of me. So now I've got more stylish ones. Designer frames in nutbrown that apparently complement my face shape.

Bringing in the bucket and lights, I place it all next to the tree, hang up my coat, take off my boots, and make my way over to him. Placing the kettle back on the side, he turns to me with a small smile that doesn't reach his eyes. Like he's just trying to be polite. There's a noticeable change in his blue eyes. They seem devoid of life, less vibrant. I'm such a piece of shit. I did that to him.

"You got it all fixed, then?" he asks, picking up the two green bowls.

"Yeah, all sorted. I'll just turn the stopcock back on under the sink and I'll be on my way."

"Well, you can't leave before you eat." He raises the bowls. "So do that, then come sit."

Once I've turned on the water supply, I make my way over to Tristan, taking a seat on the opposite side of him.

"Here, have some bread. You can use it to mop up the gravy." A plate of buttered goodness is thrust across the table. Taking three slices, I greedily start eating.

"Mmmmm, this is amazing," I moan. "Thank you," I add around mouthfuls of food. "Where did you learn to cook?"

"My mum," is all he says. He takes small bites of his food, and his shoulders are more hunched over.

"Well, if I ever meet her, I'll be sure to tell her she taught you well." I go for a tentative smile.

His left eye twitches as he bows his head and continues to eat. It's quiet while we both fill our bellies, and the weight of my mistake starts weighing heavily on me. There's a tension in the air that wasn't there before, and I don't like it. Once I've finished eating, I sit patiently waiting for Tristan to finish his, but after pushing a carrot around his bowl for the third time, I take matters into my own hands.

"Look, I'm sorry about earlier," I start. Tristan's eyes meet mine as I continue. "I didn't mean to shout at you. I dunno what came over me. But I genuinely didn't mean to hurt your feelings. Sometimes, I just speak before I think. I'm used to telling the kids at school what to do, so I guess it must've been the teacher in me. Please forgive me?" If he wants to punch me in the face right now so I can feel as hurt as he looks, then I'll gladly take the hit.

The spoon Tristan was holding drops into his bowl and he pushes it away. "It's fine," he says, his voice not relaying any emotions.

"No, it's not fine, and it's also okay if you tell me to piss off, or that I'm a complete arsehole." The last part gets a little smile from him, his lips doing a cute curl at the corners of his mouth.

He sighs. "You're not an arsehole. I... I just don't like being made to feel small. Ridiculed. Pathetic. Truth is, I was bullied at school. It just brings back all of them old feelings that I've tried so hard to overcome." The smile disappears again, and it feels like the sun has retreated behind a grey cloud.

Dickhead, I curse myself. Absolute dickhead. I finally get to be around the one person who's made me feel attraction in the longest time—maybe ever—and I blew it. Way to go, Dax. "Shit, I'm sorry. I didn't know. But that doesn't excuse my behaviour. I shouldn't have said what I did. I just saw you half-dressed out in the cold and wanted to... I dunno..." Slumping back in my chair and pushing my glasses to the top of my head, I rub my eyes.

"Protect me?" he says, his voice all frail and vulnerable.

I huff out a breath, putting my glasses back on. "Yeah, something like that." *Exactly that!* My heart thunders in my chest.

"I get it. You're a good dad and the kids you teach are lucky to have you. It's only natural that you'd be concerned." He gives me a half smile. "I'm sorry I made you feel bad because I'm sensitive."

Is he for real? *He's* apologising to *me*? Without even realising it, my hand moves across the table and clasps his in mine. Considering I usually avoid holding hands, this feels strangely right. "You have every right to feel sensitive. I shouldn't have said anything. And I'm sorry for the way you were treated in school; no one should have to go through that. Clearly, they were the real arseholes, and I hope they all have karma pay them a visit and end up with super hairy toes or smelly breath." The sound of Tristan's spontaneous laughter lights up my insides, bringing a smile to my face. That's better. I like seeing him happy.

"You're ridiculous," he frowns, the smile lingering in his eyes.

"Got you to smile, though, didn't I?" I feel terrible that I brought back bad memories for him. If I'd been in his school, I would've made all of them fuckers pay. Detention for a year. Rubbish duty in the rain. I can't stand bullies. We don't tolerate it at our school. We try to teach our kids to be good people and to raise each other up instead of putting each other down.

We're still holding hands, but I'm not going to be the one who pulls away first. This might be my only chance to experience the velvety touch of his soft skin against mine. Looking across at him now, I mentally capture every detail of his appearance; from the way his smile radiates happiness to the shimmering blue of his eyes, now that the sparkle in them is back. The scattering of freckles across his nose. The way his curls have a mind of their own, dancing and swaying with each move he makes. Adorable. There's something about his red hair and pale complexion that reminds me of a little fox. Little Fox.

He squeezes my hand. "Thank you," he murmurs.

"For what? Upsetting you?" I say as I rub my thumb over the top of his hand.

"For making me laugh. For understanding. For saying sorry."

Squeezing his hand back, I say, "Just for the record, I think you're perfect, just as you are."

Although a cute blush creeps up his neck, I instantly regret my words, knowing that even though they are sincere, they're better left unsaid. He's my son's best friend, which makes him completely off-limits.

As much as I hate to do so, I pull my hand back. The last thing he needs is me confusing him with mixed signals. The way my heart races whenever I see him is *my* issue. Not his.

Standing up, I push back my chair and grab my bowl to carry it to the dishwasher. Tristan's bare feet pad softly behind me. "I need to get going before the snowstorm gets stronger."

"Oh. Well... at least let me wrap you some cookies for the journey home. You might not have time to stop if the weather gets too bad."

See? Bloody perfect.

Taking the container, I walk towards the front door. Reluctantly, I put on my coat and slip my feet back into my damp boots. Tristan remains rooted in the same spot as earlier, his arms now tightly crossed in front of his chest, and his gaze fixated on the floor. There's a tiny ember of hope burning inside me, suggesting that he might not want me to leave after all. Because leaving is the last thing I want to do. But I have to. I *must*. "Well... I best be on my way. Thank you again for the cookies," I shrug, holding up the cookies.

"You're welcome. Thanks for fixing the leak," he says softly, something lingering in his voice that I can't quite decipher.

Even now, he refuses to make eye contact, his toes sinking into the softness of the thick rug. What was I expecting? That he would throw himself at me and beg me to stay?

"Take care of yourself, Tristan."

His small voice only just reaches my ears. "You, too."

Before I do something crazy like throw caution to the wind and kiss him, I pull the door open. A powerful gust of wind grabs the door and flings it open, banging on the cabin wall, revealing a spectacular snowstorm and the untamed force of Mother Nature. Shit, I've left it too late. There's no way I can drive home in that blizzard. The snow is so thick that it blankets everything in sight, obscuring the view beyond the porch.

I grab the door and slam it shut, turning towards Tristan just in time to notice an enormous smile stretching across his face. It seems almost too perfect to be a coincidence; if I didn't know any better,

I would think he had intentionally arranged this. "Guess I'm not going anywhere tonight," I sigh.

"Oh no, what a shame." He blinks. Turning, he heads to the kitchen with a sway to his hips. I'm so screwed. It's fine, I try to tell myself. It's just one night. I can keep my hands to myself.

It's. Just. One. Night.

Chapter Eight

MY HAPPY LITTLE HEART is racing as I thoroughly wash up the *one* spoon in the sink. A mix of exhilaration at the prospect of spending more time with Dax and the anxiety of concealing my feelings for him in such close quarters are fighting against each other inside me. I'm still processing the impact of his hand gently gripping mine had on me. It was such a small gesture, but it was the first time anyone had ever caressed my hand in a soothing way aside from Mum. It wasn't related to anything sexual; it was... nice.

Yes, I've had many guys treat me nicely, but only because they wanted to have sex with me. Dax showed genuine concern, not pity. I can't help but wonder how my life might have been different if he had been around to frighten off my bullies. Could Dax's presence have prevented my self-loathing and kept my dark thoughts at bay? Maybe. Probably not. But like my therapist said, 'Each moment in life paves the way for the next chapter. Confront your fears head-on, and you might be pleasantly surprised by the person you become.'

Dax being snowed in here for at least tonight is a sign for me to say *fuck it*. I want him. From the very first time I saw Dax walk through those doors that night, I've been attracted to him. It would be a missed opportunity not to find out if he feels the same way.

It's brat-unleashing time.

Turning round, Dax has taken off his coat and boots, and he almost looks like a deer caught in the headlights, standing there with his hands in his jeans pockets, looking a little unsure. Oh, my sweet Dax, you have *no* idea.

"So," I say, walking towards him. "Seeing as you're staying, let's decorate the tree before we have a death on our hands." I bite my lip for effect.

He rubs his hands down his jeans like maybe he has sweaty palms. I hope he does. Do I make him nervous? I hope I do. "Yeah, okay, we could do that," he replies.

"Great, let me just get my balls out." A choking sound comes from Dax. "Oops, I mean my baubles. You didn't think I meant these balls, did you?" I say, cupping mine. His eyes go wide. I'm sure I hear a muffled '*Jesus*' as he walks over to the tree. Tris 1, Dax 0.

After going into the bedroom and grabbing the bag with all the different-coloured baubles I picked up from the market, I head back into the living room to find Dax on all fours in front of the tree. He's placing big rocks inside the green bucket he brought inside. It's the second time today he's been in that position, and I'm not mad about it. To be frank, I could comfortably sit on the arm of the sofa and indulge in thoughts of all the explicit things I would be willing to let him do to me. "Do you need any help?" I ask, coming to stand next to him.

"Imnrlydone."

"What was that?" I chuckle.

Sitting back on his calves, he looks up at me. "It's okay. I'm done. She's sturdy." He nods towards the tree.

Raising my eyebrows, I muse, "She? You mean him."

He looks at the tree, then back at me with one sexy-as-hell raised eyebrow. "Him?"

"Yeah, Mr Spruce. He'll be handsome once we've finished decorating him. C'mon, let's get started. I think some Christmas songs are needed to get us into the spirit of things." I hit *Play* on my phone and put it on the small side table next to the sofa. '*Snowman*' by Sia starts to play. Dax is my very own snowman and I'm gonna thaw him up with all my love bombing.

Going straight in with the important question, I say, "So, Dax, do you have a partner?" Picking up the emerald-green bauble, I pretend to inspect it, so I don't need to make eye contact with him. I need to know if he's off-limits or not. I'm no home-wrecker.

"Excuse me?" he croaks.

"You know, a partner? Boyfriend? Fiancé?"

With a sigh, he shakes his head and reaches down to pick up a string of lights. "If you must know," he says, his eyes meeting mine as he turns to face me. "The answer is no. No partner. Relationships are not my thing." Turning towards the tree again, he starts to wrap the lights around its branches.

Noted. I'll have to work harder than I thought. "Who pissed in your cornflakes to make you not want to have a relationship?"

His laughter fills the room, bright and warm, like sunbeams. "I can see why Jake loves you."

Knock me over with a feather, won't you? The beauty of this man is undeniable, from his handsome face to his charming smile. *I want him so badly.* Santa, if you could do me a solid and give me Dax, I promise I'll continue being a good boy.

If I'm not careful, I'll be in a situation where I have to change my shorts. Since I don't wear underwear, there's a high chance that if I get a hard-on and blow my load, Dax will definitely notice. I would rather he be a participant than a spectator. "Yeah? Why's that?" I ask.

Balancing on his tiptoes, he reaches up to secure the last of the lights at the top of the tree. My eyes are fixed on him as his shirt slowly exposes the smooth skin on the side of his body, leaving me practically drooling. Fuck, I'm getting hard. *Down boy.* I try to stop my erection in its tracks by pushing on the front of my shorts.

"Your fun nature makes you a joy to be around. You have a straightforward approach, yet there is a gentle sweetness that radiates from you. Not to mention, you're kind-hearted. You're a good person, Tris."

Tris. I love the way he sometimes slips up and accidentally calls me by that nickname. And his words make me want to cry happy tears. Despite only spending a few hours together, he has already picked up on these aspects of my personality. It has taken me a considerable amount of time to come to the realisation that I am inherently good, despite the negative self-image my mind often projects.

How did I go from being on the brink of orgasm to feeling a strong urge to cry? Talk about a rollercoaster of emotions.

Once Dax finishes with the lights, we decorate the tree with the balls. No matter how hard I try, I can't stretch my arms high enough to reach the upper branches. To overcome the disadvantages of being five-foot-six, Dax fetches a small step stool from the laundry room. *My hero.*

With a sense of nostalgia, I place the last ball, a bright purple one, near the top of the tree, honouring my mum's favourite colour in the absence of an angel. Just as I step back to admire my work, I lose my balance. "Shit," I blurt.

Just as I try to steady myself, strong hands wrap around my waist, keeping me upright. We're back to being skin-to-skin, and my body immediately starts buzzing.

"Careful." The whisper of his words tickles my ear, sending goosebumps down my spine.

As I lean against Dax, I can't help but be warmed by the heat emanating from his hands and body, kindling a small flame of contentment within me. Determined to do whatever it takes to keep the flame burning, I take a gradual step down to ensure Dax continues to hold on to me. I don't want him to let me go just yet.

"So," he says, taking a moment to clear his throat before continuing. "How about you? Any partner? Boyfriend? Fiancé?"

Glancing over my shoulder at him, I shake my head. "No. Not yet. Still waiting for my special someone," I bat my eyelashes. Dax releases his grip on me and takes a step back. Despite feeling the loss of him, I can't help but be pleased with how the tree turned out, even with the lights not switched on yet.

"Yeah? What does '*special someone*' entail?" He frowns adorably.

My gaze lingers on the tree. "Oh, you know, the usual things. Someone who sees all my flaws and loves me, anyway."

I glance over at Dax, standing beside me now, his feet shuffling restlessly and his forehead etched with frown lines. Did I manage to make him feel uncomfortable again? I reach out and touch his arm. "You all right? You're not stroking on me, are you? Cos I'll happily give you CPR."

Lifting his head to look at me, he chuckles, "I'm good. Let's get these lights turned on."

My hand falls from his arm as he walks over to the switch on the wall. Whatever he was thinking about has dispersed.

"Ready?" he asks.

"Wait!" I shout, rushing over to my phone. "We need the right song." The smooth notes of '*Christmas Tree*' sung by Teddy Swims sets the tone. "Okay ready. Light up Mr Spruce."

The warm white lights glow softly. The tree stands tall against the cabin wall, its branches adorned with a beautiful assortment of coloured balls, creating a truly perfect sight.

As we both gaze at our handiwork, Dax stands beside me, a satisfied smile on his face. "Well, isn't that something? Mr Spruce really is a handsome tree."

Fuck. My heart is bursting. He really loves our tree. *Our* tree. Armed with my phone, I take a few photos, making it a point to capture some candid shots of us together. Not gonna lie; the picture of Dax standing by the tree is going to be my bedtime buddy tonight.

Chapter Nine

TRISTAN HAS BEEN HUFFING and puffing away in the bedroom for over an hour. Lying on the sofa, my makeshift bed for the night, I can hear his frustrated murmurs. At least ten times, I've been tempted to go in there and ask him what's troubling him. But I held strong. I'm better off staying away from him. The more time I spend with him, the stronger my attraction becomes. My self-control reached its peak this evening. Countless times, I had to clench my fist tightly to resist the temptation of touching him. I held up my palms, inspecting them. Yep, those were definitely nail imprints, clear as day. But I just have to keep reminding myself that I am not someone who gets involved in relationships, especially not with my son's best friend.

With all the lights turned off, it's just me and the flickering fire. The familiar sounds of the fireplace popping and crackling, which usually bring me comfort, cannot calm my restless mind tonight. I've spent many nights on the sofa throughout the years, but I can't quite seem to settle. My stomach feels like it's tied up in knots. With one arm tucked under my head and the spare blanket draped over me, I gaze up at the beam stretching across the cabin. The estate agent thought I was crazy when I told her to find me something I could fix up.

"But Mr Brooker, we have plenty of cabins that are all ready and perfectly furnished. Why don't I show you them?"

My eyes didn't waver as I told her, "If you can't find me what I'm asking for, then I'll find someone who can."

"Oh no, no, Mr Brooker, I'll find you what you want," she said through her fake smile and gritted teeth.

Two weeks later, I was heading out here. The memory of my first visit to this cabin twenty-one years ago still lingers in my mind. Pulling up outside, the untamed vegetation had taken over completely, obscuring the exterior of the cabin. Opening the door, a musty scent of damp wood filled the air, tainted by the faint odour of rot. The windows, showing signs of age, could no longer keep the rainwater out. Countless holes marked the main beam, worn and weathered, left behind by the woodworm. It was too far gone to save, so it was the first thing I changed. The run-down condition of the place was exactly what I had been searching for—a project that I could restore and pour my love into. Rough around the edges, but sturdy. Something that was mine.

It lacked the opulence of the big house my parents had helped us buy years ago, right before Jake was about to be born. This purchase definitely did *not* meet with my mother's approval. But if I was going to accept my parents' birthday gift, I'd made it clear this place was what I wanted. I needed this cabin.

I cherish my little sanctuary, a place of tranquillity, far removed from the chaos of daily existence. Summers with Jake made the rest of the year bearable as we filled them with laughter and adventure. It's definitely been lonelier without him these past few years, but I hope one day Jake will bless me with grandchildren who will have the opportunity to grow up in this place as well.

I direct my body towards the sofa, take off my glasses, and close my eyes in an effort to try to sleep.

And then I hear it. The soft *pad-pad-pad* of Tristan's feet. I can't see him, but I know he's there.

"What's wrong?"

The next thing I know, he has laid himself on the sofa, his slim frame finding its way snugly up against mine, creating a perfect fit behind me. What the hell?

"I'm cold. I can't sleep when I'm cold." The constant chattering of his teeth interrupts his words. Fuck, he really is freezing. I should have added more logs to the fire. I dare not move, though, as I feel his cool body pressed against my bare skin.

"Umm, maybe you could put a jumper on?" I suggest, trying to distance myself from him, fighting the temptation to roll over and embrace his body, providing him with the warmth he craves.

"Don't have one," he shivers.

If I close my eyes, I can pretend this is all just a dream. A wonderful, tempting one, but just a dream. "Borrow one of mine?"

I feel the warmth of his breath against my neck when he speaks. "I'll get too hot. I can't sleep when I'm hot, either."

What is this? *Goldilocks and the Three Bears*? Too hot, too cold! Except in my story, he takes on the role of the defenceless little red fox, while I become the ravenous wolf, eager to consume him.

After a couple of minutes of him restlessly shifting behind me, inadvertently pressing himself against my back and me attempting to block out any thoughts about the placement of his dick, I decide we can't stay like this. There's simply not enough room for both of us to get a good night's sleep here. I need space. He's making it difficult for me to maintain self-control and not touch him.

"Tris?"

"Yeah."

"Let's get you back to bed."

"I'm only going if you come with me. You're toasty warm and I already feel sleepy. I didn't sleep well last night either."

Bloody hell.

"C'mon, get up." As he moans and stands up, I shiver as a gust of cool air brushes against my back, a stark reminder of the absence of his skin touching me. Pushing myself up into a sitting position, I quickly spin around, my feet connecting with the solid wooden floor. I slide my glasses back onto my face, and there, in front of me, is Tristan, looking elegant in his cream silk pyjamas. Shorts and a short-sleeved button-up top, leaving very little to the imagination. His curly hair is even more untamed. The fire behind him lights up his figure, making him look positively stunning.

Fuck me.

I want him in a way that makes my heart race and my palms sweat. I *crave* him. As I take in every inch of him, I imagine how his naked body would look, creamy and inviting, sprawled on the rug beneath him.

Tristan rubs his bare arms, reminding me he's cold.

"Let's go," I grit.

Thankfully, he obediently follows my instructions and quietly returns to the bedroom. I move stealthily behind him, taking the opportunity to rearrange myself subtly without him catching on.

I pull back the cover and gently pat the bed. "Hop in."

Tris hurries over to the side of the bed, but before getting in, he looks up at me with a questioning gaze. "You're getting in too, right?"

There's something enchanting about the pools of his deep blue eyes that draw me in. My nod instantly brightens his sleepy face with delight. He eagerly leaps onto the bed, pulling the soft covers up to his neck. I tenderly tuck the cover around him, ensuring that he's shielded from the chilly air. With just his head on the pillow, he looks as snug as a bug. As I walk to the other side of the bed, I feel his sleepy, seductive gaze following my every move.

After settling myself as far away from him as humanly possible, I take a deep breath and feel a wave of relief wash over me. This is fine. It's all good. I can be beside him in a way that allows him to sleep peacefully. It's a good deed that I'm doing. I'm just doing what a good housemate should do. Anybody else would have done the same. It's only natural to want your friend to be happy. Yeah, friends,

I can be his friend. I'll just wait until he drifts off to sleep, and then I'll quietly slip back to the couch.

The soft glow of the side lamp disappears as Tris reaches over and switches it off, leaving the room in utter darkness. The bed is being bumped and jiggled by his constant shifting. Frustrated, he lets out a sigh and fidgets. Tossing and turning, he thumps his pillows, desperately trying to find a comfortable spot.

Another sigh escapes my lips. This one is throwing in the towel. The one where I know I've given in. I have shattered my own boundaries. Tris needs comfort. I can feel it deep in my bones.

"Come here," I murmur.

In the blink of an eye, he's by my side. Curling up against my chest, he nuzzles me with the tenderness of a small animal burrowing into a cosy nest. It's not terrible. My arm gently rests across his waist, contouring to his every curve. I feel the gentle tickle of his contented sigh against the hair on my chest. Then come the gentle snores. The tension slowly dissipates from my body, leaving me feeling relaxed. The knot in my stomach is gone.

I don't do the whole staying-over thing with my hookups. We fuck, then we go our separate ways. It's a rule I always abide by—no exceptions—because there's an undeniable intimacy in falling asleep with someone. I don't do that. Intimacy. But here I am. With Tris. And I don't think I've felt this at peace in well... ever. What is this man doing to me?

I'm so fucked.

Chapter Ten

Nothing beats the smell of bacon. I've been up since the butt crack of dawn. My hard-on wouldn't quit. Even though I didn't want to leave Dax's comforting embrace, the pain in my cock was becoming unbearable. I don't think he would appreciate waking up to me whacking one off in the bed next to him. We're not there yet! After quickly grabbing one of my wrapped presents, I hopped into the shower, had a wank, and then decided to make him breakfast. I still find it hard to believe that he slept in the same bed as me. It felt natural, and I certainly slept better.

The change in the environment was quite drastic for me. Coming from a street on a busy road filled with the sound of sirens and people passing by, it was a shock to experience complete silence while sleeping here. The occasional howl of an animal only heightened the fear that it might crash through the window and attack me. The lack of sleep was finally starting to take its toll on me last night. I was tossing and turning and getting on my own nerves, so I got up to get some warm milk, but Dax practically told me to come lie down with him. That's my story at least, and I'm sticking to it.

Yes, I could have put on one of his cardigans when my teeth chattered like a lively mariachi band. I won't admit or deny wearing one and pleasuring myself in it on the first night. But my intention was simply to have a drink and then return to bed. There was an undeniable pull towards him I couldn't ignore, no matter how much I tried. So, I invaded his personal space. He smelled absolutely divine, too. His naturally warm smell and the hint of teak are fast becoming my favourite scents.

I promise that the only reason I was rubbing up against his back was to get warm. I soon realised that it took little to make Dax give in to my plea to sleep in the same bed. Although I think today he might be back on track with the '*deny-Tris-sex*' train. I'm too cute to be this under-fucked, so I plan on being myself today with a touch of extra flirt.

My outfit for today comprises my baby-blue shorts, which I'm wearing commando because nuts need to breathe, people, and a knitted blue crop top featuring dainty white snowflakes. It was one of my gifts to myself. Now that the Christmas tree is up, I've put the rest of my presents underneath it, and I plan to open one every day. It's unfortunate that Dax doesn't have any gifts, but I hope he'll still appreciate mine. Good thing I don't mind sharing them.

The cabin is now bathed in bright light as the blinds are pulled up, revealing a landscape of glistening snow outside. This morning, I couldn't help but do a happy dance when I looked outside and realised that Dax couldn't go home.

Just as I finish dishing up the bacon and eggs, Dax saunters into the living room, clad in his baggy, red cotton PJ bottoms. Damn, he looks even hotter in the morning sun. The warmth of that fuzzy chest kept me comfortable throughout the night.

"Nice shirt," I smirk as he walks over to me.

His face creases with a frown as he looks down at his bare chest. "Oh um. That's what I came to ask. Do you know where my T-shirts are? They're not on the shelf."

I hold in my smirk and try not to let my mind wander to the thought of sucking on his nips. Additionally, I won't mention that I hid all his shirts last night, secretly hoping he would spend the rest of his stay shirtless.

Clearing my throat. "I moved them to the bottom drawer 'cause I needed room for my things. I had no idea you would be staying here as well. Sorry," I hum, giving what I hope is my innocent face.

"Oh, yeah. Makes sense," he says, scratching his head.

Some people might hesitate or feel ashamed to admit that they think about their crush more than what is considered 'normal,' but not me. I'm different! I'll tell anyone who'll listen that Dax and his hot-as-fuck cardigans feature in all my sex dreams, and in all my jack-off sessions! Dax is all I think about! He's got those broad shoulders that would look great flexing when he throws me over them. As his light scruff grows, I can't help but imagine the red trail marks it would leave on my pale body as he licks me from head to toe. His plump pink lips that I often picture around my cock, swallowing me down as I tug on his messy hair.

The way he carries himself, all proper like the teacher he is, but under his clothes he hides this body that I'm desperate to get my hands on. I just need a little taste of him, then I'll be able to put him out of my mind. Yeah, right, who am I kidding? I want to burrow inside him and live there forever.

Dax stands there, his eyes scanning me up and down. That's right, take a good look, and see what you're missing out on. His eyes go wide when he spots the unmistakable bulge in my shorts. Taking slow steps, I move closer to him, my lower lip caught between my teeth as I fondle myself. He can't take his eyes off me. Hmm, things are looking up. Screw it, I'm seizing the moment and making my move with him because life is too short. I didn't earn the title of brat for nothing.

"Eyes up here, Daddy."

"What?" he splutters and clears his throat, his eyes now looking at me and not my dick, which is a shame. Stopping just in front of him, he stammers, "I... I'm not your daddy, so don't call me that."

Oh, he *definitely* likes that. The rosy hue on his cheeks is evidence enough.

"Mhm, ok. Want me to call you something different? Perhaps... sir?"

My finger traces a path down his chest until it reaches the waistband of his pyjamas, and I can't help but pop out my bottom lip while locking eyes with him. He swallows hard. Stepping back, he rubs his face. It's clear that I have an effect on him. I know he wants me, but he's too stubborn to admit it. I know men. I can read them like a book. He wants to board the Tristan train. Just buy a ticket, hot stuff, and you can hop on and off all day.

The chances of him deciding that we'll be together forever are about the same odds as him dropping to his knees right now and deep-throating me like he does in my dreams. But I'm nothing if not determined.

I see the pulse in his neck ticking. I'm not sure if it's working overtime from lust running through him at seeing me in so little or if I'm just stressing him the fuck out. Right now, all I can think about is the way I want to run my tongue along his neck and discover if he tastes as delicious as I imagine. And now I'm rock hard... again.

"I'm, er, just gonna go get changed." He throws his thumb behind him, then spins on his sock-covered feet and makes a dash for the bedroom.

"Don't be too long," I call out. "I made you breakfast. They say the best way to a man's heart is through his stomach." Or his butt hole in my case.

Dax is hiding outside. He's been clearing the snow off the porch. Trying to distract myself, I spend the morning making blueberry muffins and cooking a shepherd's pie for dinner. I even did some washing, but with nothing left to do, I dumped myself on the couch and I'm currently ogling him through the window. Grunts and the relentless thud of the axe against wood are the only noises breaking the silence.

Dax initially had on a large coat, but it appears he sweated so much that he no longer has it on. I mean, who does he think he is walking around in that 100% Aaron knit cardigan, throwing out pheromones like candy? I had to go have my second wank of the day just so my hard-on would go away.

As I watch him outside, I know round three with my cock is imminent. I can't be responsible for my libido when he's doing a Justin Timberlake on me and '*bringing sexy back*.' You hear that song and the first thing you wanna do is dance around a pole and slut drop! I'm more than happy to have Dax as my pole. He can be my North Pole. I'll even wear a Santa hat!

A few hours have gone by, and I'm now officially bored. Since Dax is still outside, I decide to plate up a couple of muffins and bring him a cup of tea. I'm sure he's trying to turn himself into a snowman out there. He must be freezing. Do we even need that much wood? It seems like he's making every effort to steer clear of being in this space with me. I have news for him—I'm not going anywhere. I throw on my jacket, boots, and Trixy hat, leaving my legs bare, and head out to bug him.

"Hey! I thought you might be hungry, so I brought you some tea and a snack. Don't want you wasting away out here," I joke.

Taking off his gloves, he smiles as he accepts the plate from me and places it on top of the wood storage. Handing over the warm cup, I retrieve my muffin from my pocket while he takes a sip.

"Thank you for this." The cold air causes his warm breath to turn into smoke.

"I wasn't sure if you were trying to avoid me." Trying to flirt with him, I run my finger across my bottom lip, a gesture that never fails to attract guys. It reminds them of how a mouth feels around their cocks. When I release my wet lip, it pops on my top lip. Dax doesn't seem too impressed, but then he turns and I'm pretty sure he's fixing himself in his corduroys.

"I'm not avoiding you," he says, his back still turned. "I'm just keeping busy."

Frustrated, I realise I'm making zero progress with Dax. He's like a brick wall, so I silence myself by devouring my muffin, dropping crumbs on my coat. The wheels have come off the track, and Dax has disembarked. Just like that, all the progress I thought I'd made has disappeared into thin air. Maybe this is all just a fruitless endeavour. What could he possibly find interesting in someone like me? The only thing he sees is his son's friend. A silly kid with a crush.

It started off as a crush, but now I'm questioning whether my feelings for Dax have deepened. This is the first time I've ever been so emotionally invested in a guy. There's just something about him that calls to me on some deeper level.

Looking out at the beautiful snow-covered forest, I tear chunks off the muffin and enjoy the sweet burst of blueberries in my mouth. Once I'm finished, I turn around to find Dax staring at me. This tension between us is off the charts. I can feel it. I don't care how much he tries to ignore this thing between us; I know he feels it, too. The sparks might be invisible, but they're there.

There's a crumb on the side of Dax's lip, and I can't help myself as I take a step closer to him, reaching out with my thumb and sliding it into his mouth. He maintains eye contact as he sucks on my thumb. I hold in my gasp as his warm, wet mouth latches on to me. My throbbing erection strains against its restraints, desperate for release. Just as I think he might grab my coat, pull me close and kiss the fuck out of me, he pulls away and picks up his axe like the moment didn't happen. What the fuck is happening?

In my mind, everything is a chaotic mess, like ingredients in a mixing bowl. Churning, but not quite coming together. I know he wants me as much as I want him. His eyes reveal everything to me. He attempts to conceal it, but the undeniable desire practically emanates from him. I'm not sure why he's hesitating to take what he wants from me. I refuse to let him see the mix of emotions swirling inside me—confusion, sadness, and anger. Spinning on my heels, I go back inside. Well, screw him. And screw his handsome face and hairy chest and... and.... his cardigan.

He might not want to fuck me, but he can damn well listen to me fuck myself.

Dax is my catnip, one sniff of him and I'm high as a fucking kite, off my tits, up in the clouds. Slamming the front door, I throw my coat on the floor and fling off my boots. Stomping into the bedroom, I open the window just enough that he can hear me, but not enough to freeze my bollocks off.

My shorts are gone, and my cock, with its little curve, stands at attention. Leaving my jumper on, I reach for the lube in the bedside drawer. Sprawled on the bed, I cover my fingers with gel and insert one into my needy hole. "*Ahhhh, fuck yes.*" This is what I needed. I continue to finger fuck myself, getting louder and louder till I hear the door slam shut.

Shortly after, in the bedroom doorway, stands the big bad wolf, its chest heaving as he stares at me.

"Do you want to watch, or are you interested in joining me? I'm fine with either option," I pant.

I playfully taunt him while shamelessly thrusting my fingers in and out. I know he likes what he sees. From my vantage point, I can observe his jaw twitching and his fists tightly clenched. Inside that gorgeous head of his, he is engaged in a fierce internal battle. He wants me. Slowly, I run my tongue along my palm before moving it to my cock, stroking up and down. As his resolve weakens, it's like watching cracks spread across the body of a fragile porcelain doll.

"All you have to do is come over here, D," I say, and a faint whimper drifts from the other side of the room. I spread my legs apart before bending my legs towards my head. Now he has a clear view of the goods, my tight hole tempting him like a siren's call.

It was a step too far, though. He abruptly turns and exits the room, leaving me to hear the front door open, followed by an unearthly scream. I'm worried I broke him, but I don't stop touching myself. I can't.

Tris 2, Dax 0.

Chapter Eleven

"*Fuuuuuuuccccckkkkkk.*" The sound of my scream reverberates through the untouched wilderness. The trees bounce my voice back to me like a pathetic echo. Even though I already knew what Tristan had been doing indoors, I needed to confirm it by seeing it with my own eyes. On the bed, he lay with his fingers buried deep inside his arse. Not a care in the world as he fucked himself. I couldn't take it; I had to leave to compose myself so I wouldn't jump him like Horny Santa.

My heart is racing so fast that I can feel it throbbing in my head. I'm mad at myself for going in there, but I'm also so damn turned on that it hurts. I've been hard all day. I thought braving the freezing cold would get rid of it, but apparently, my dick was just as stubborn as Tristan.

I resisted the urge to release my load when he unexpectedly inserted his thumb into my mouth, which was a challenging moment for me, but I remained composed and did not give in to the temptation.

I could feel him chipping away at my defences, unravelling me like an onion, exposing one layer at a time until I was completely powerless against him. I'm left now with the bare bones of my being, watching my resolve crumble before me.

Should I give in to my desire and finally act on the attraction I've felt for him for so long? My son's best friend. We're both adults here. Tris has been so forward about his attraction to me; it's like he's leaving a trail of breadcrumbs for me to follow. Those shorts he wears would try the patience of a saint.

I walk back and forth, attempting to release my frustration by running my hands through my hair. He's a little shit. He shouldn't be tempting a man who's clearly weak. I should have known better than to stay and should have just driven away in my car during the raging storm. *But you didn't want to leave, did you?*

Pausing my restless movement, I grasp the railing on the porch, the sensation of the cold snow on my fingers bringing me back to the here and now. I'm a full-blooded man who has needs, damn it. Amid my inner conflict, I feel a gentle bubbling sensation growing in my belly. Fuck, am I nervous? The simple answer is *yes*.

Suddenly, a sound reaches my ears, the sound of Tris's moaning filling the air. While I was having a mini freakout, the little shit didn't even bother to stop playing with himself.

I feel a tug-of-war between my body and my mind as I walk towards the door. It's a reckless, foolish, and terrible decision. He's strictly off-limits. *Keep telling yourself that.* However, all those things are inconsequential now. He exposed himself to me. And I want him. I'm desperate for my little fox.

Without even thinking, I automatically remove all my clothing except for my trousers as I make my way to the bedroom.

Spread open on the bed are slim but muscular legs, with feet resting gently on the soft mattress. His hard cock rests in his neatly trimmed pubes. I can see he's leaking even from here; clear liquid has gathered in a pool on his stomach, trailing into his goddamn belly button. His pink asshole is inviting me to come play. It's glistening and puffy from his touch. My many attempts to picture this in my mind pale compared to actually witnessing it. I'm salivating.

Tristan's fingers teasingly move back to his needy hole.

Not happening. As I step closer to the bed, I quickly slap away his greedy hand.

"Ouch! What was that for?" A pout is visible on his face. My fingers itch to spank the brat out of him, but I think he would enjoy it too much.

"This... now belongs to me." There is no mistaking my seriousness, as my voice carries a deep and demanding tone. He wanted me to cave, and now that I have, I'm taking ownership of what is mine. "I'm gonna wreck you, Tris, consume all of you. Fuck you till I've had my fill. You've driven me to madness, and now you'll take everything I have to give."

A soft whimper escapes his lips, breaking the stillness of the room. That's what I figured. He knows who's in control now. *Me.*

My thoughts are like a raging storm. I spent years building the walls that now surround me, perfecting my hookups to meet my needs. Letting no one in. Yet, twenty-four hours with Tris and all the walls I've built around myself have come crashing down. He has shaken even the foundation.

Surrounded by my wreckage, I ask, "Are you sure this is what you want?"

"Yes." His breathy voice signals his want, but the fire in his eyes is my permission to go ahead.

With a gentle touch, I trace the inside of his leg with the back of my hand until I reach his groin. The feeling of goosebumps on his skin under my touch brings a sense of delight. The sound of Tris's breathy moans is adding fuel to the fire raging within me.

"Protection?" I croak, my voice hoarse.

"I'm on PrEP."

That makes me happy. I wouldn't normally go in bare, but with Tris, I need to. There's a deep-seated feeling in my gut that needs to be filled with the feel of him. Until I've thoroughly explored every detail of his body and his taste lingers on my taste buds, I won't be satisfied.

"Me too," I rasp as I unfasten my trousers and watch as they drop to the floor. "Lube?" I question as I step out of them. The only thing standing between us now are my black *Calvin's*.

"Here," he struggles with his slippery hands, finally handing me the sleek, black bottle of *pjur*. My favourite type of lube: silicone-based. I slide my underwear down, nice and easy. I'm pleased to see the anticipation on his face. His eyes widen and he moistens his lips with excitement. Now it's his time to suffer. To be *teased*.

Just as my pubes become visible, I pause and grin to myself. His open mouth quickly morphs into a snarl, accompanied by a deep frown on his face. It's no fun being on the receiving end, is it?

Resting on his forearms, he gazes at me through the space between his open legs. Slowly, I continue sliding my briefs down until I'm completely naked. My cock springs back and hits my stomach. There's a seductive glint dancing in his eyes that I want to spend forever looking at. *Forever.* Hmm, that's an unfamiliar word for me.

"What the... what are *those*?"

Oh, he spotted the beads right away. The hidden secret I keep. It never fails to impress. While I typically give my partners a heads-up about them, I find myself fascinated by the aura of curiosity radiating from Tris.

As he attempts to sit up for a better view, I firmly push him back down. "Little fox, did I give you permission to move?"

"But..."

Butts will definitely play a part in this. With a raised brow, I communicate a subtle warning. Like a moody teenager, he lays back down with a pout on his face. I love how he surrenders his control to me.

"It's called pearling," I say as I gently tug his legs towards the edge of the bed. "Their purpose is to give you pleasure."

"Is this gonna hurt?" he asks, a hint of concern clear in his expression.

Leaning over his body, I look him directly in the eye. "I promise you, little fox, I will never harm you. If there's anything I do you don't like, just let me know, and I'll stop."

As he contemplates my words, I watch attentively, waiting for him to make a decision.

"Okay," he breathes out. "I trust you."

My heart feels like it's about to burst out of my chest when those three little words are spoken. *I trust you.*

Leaning down, I delicately catch one of his pink nipples with my teeth. Using just the right amount of pressure, I bite him, causing a moan to escape his lips, before soothing the pain with a lick. I repeat the process with his other nipple before getting to my feet. As I drop to the ground, I marvel at his rosebud, tightly clenched in anticipation of what's to come. Grumbling with appreciation, I can't help but admire the view laid out before me. I succumb to temptation because that's the essence of Tris. Temptation. The smell of his arousal fills the air as I part his cheeks, intensifying my desire. I press my tongue flat against the surface of his skin and take a lick. From hole to taint. I'm done for. Just one taste and I'm hooked. My new addiction. *Tristan.*

With a combination of circular massage, gentle caresses, teasing bites, and sucking, I make him squirm until he's relaxed, allowing me to explore further with my tongue. In the throes of passion, he instinctively grasps his cheeks and pulls them apart further. A silent request. That's it, little fox, open up for me. The deeper I go, the more he craves.

"Please, Dax. I need you inside me."

The rough, throaty sound of his plea makes me jump to my feet, not even bothering to wipe the saliva from my face. I want to taste him on my tongue as I bury myself inside. Coating my fingers with lube, I insert two. With each gentle touch on his sweet spot, I coax moan after moan from him. Once I'm satisfied he's ready, I retract my fingers and use the remaining lube on my hand to cover my shaft.

"Slide back up the bed and place a pillow under your lower back for me."

Once more, he obeys my command without hesitation. Mixed emotions course through my body, with arousal at the forefront and nervousness not far behind. "Are you absolutely certain you want this?" I ask as I settle onto the bed, positioning myself between his legs.

"Absolutely, without a doubt. I've dreamt of this moment; never thought it would happen. So yes, I want this. I want you to take what you need from me. Please." The words come out clipped, his arousal getting the better of him.

I respond with a small nod. My heart races as I position myself, ready to enter his waiting body. Slowly, I push forward, the tension building as I breach him. The way he takes in a sharp breath makes me suspect he's anxious. "Relax, little fox, I'll go slow," I whisper encouragingly. "You're doing so well."

Moving in inch by inch, I feel the beads gliding inside him as he pushes back, granting me access to his body. The soft, silky walls gently wrap around my cock and he lets out a gasp as I slowly pull out an inch before sliding back in. I repeat the motion until I can fully withdraw, effortlessly sliding in and out. He takes me so fucking good.

"You're amazing, little fox. Does it feel good?"

"Yessss," he lets out in a quivering voice. "So good. Please fuck me harder. I won't break."

"Fuck, you feel so good, so warm. I knew you'd open for me."

Wrapping my arms around each of his legs, I bend them back as I pick up speed. Sweat beads on my brow. Adrenaline and lust course through my veins, creating a sensation unlike anything else. What is Tristan doing that's causing me to feel this way? Why does it feel so different with him? My movements become more deliberate as I rotate my pelvis, watching his pretty, pale body flush with a soft pink colour. He is truly a sight to behold. Tris grips my arms, trying to make me go deeper, and I just chuckle. "Be patient."

"I can't," he groans. "I need to come, but please don't stop. I feel amazing, Dax. You make me feel incredible. Why did we wait so long?"

Both of us know the answer, yet I choose to enjoy the moment and not spoil it by replying. "Take your pretty cock for me, Tris, and come with my name on your lips so you don't forget who owns you right now."

I'm so close. My dick is swelling and throbbing, begging for release, but I won't. Tris must come before anything else.

"Fuck... I'm so close, Dax, keep fucking me just like that. Ahhh. Yes. I'm... I'm coming. *Daaaaxxxx*."

Watching his release, every fibre of my being feels alive as his cum sprays across his chest. As I give in to pleasure, bursts of white light flash behind my closed eyes while I lose myself at that moment with Tristan. I release all of myself into him. Our bodies tremble with pleasure as we both reach the peak of ecstasy. I don't think I've ever had such a powerful climax. I pull out of him gently, secretly weeping the loss of him. Exhausted, I drop onto the bed next to him; the mattress offering a welcome respite. Spent. Euphoric. Knackered.

As my body gradually relaxes, and my breathing calms, worry and panic begin to creep in. I just crossed a line by being intimate with someone I was supposed to avoid. Did I just screw up? Have I shattered the trust my son has in me? What about his bond with Tris? Fuck. Fuck. *Fuck*.

Chapter Twelve

Wow. I JUST EXPERIENCED the most mind-blowing sexual encounter of my life. Dax, the hero of my imagination who can tackle frozen pipes and rocks a cape, just made me feel supercalifragilistic-expialidocious with his mind-blowing sex. He thoroughly fucked me into... wait, what day is it? I don't even know anymore. And those beads surprised me with how good they felt.

At first, I wasn't sure if his cock and balls were going to fit inside me. Dax and I were similar in size, but he looked thicker, and those beads definitely added some extra bulk. Despite Dax's reassurance, I was still wary that they might hurt, but to my surprise, they felt amazing. The small beads felt larger than they were, but they hit all the right spots perfectly.

Pearling is a new discovery for me and one I hope I get the chance to experience again. My body feels thoroughly fucked, but instead of revelling in this moment, worry starts to creep in. With Dax's warm cum still inside me, I sense the tension emanating from him. His eyes are fixed on the ceiling as I roll my head to the side and squeeze his hand.

I always dreamt and wished for this day, but never expected it to actually happen. But now that it has, I'm not sure what to do next. What is the proper procedure for sleeping with your best friend's dad? I really hope he doesn't end up regretting this. If he says that, I might end up in tears.

"Dax?"

"Shit Tris," he replies, squeezing my hand back. "We probably shouldn't have done that." He turns to face me.

Crap, he's gonna say it and break my heart.

"That's bullshit, and you know it," I bark out in defence. I try to pull my hand away, but he holds me tight.

"Don't pull away, please. I don't know what to do here, Tris. What are you thinking?"

That you make me feel so alive in a way I've never experienced before. That I've wanted this for a long time, and it was every bit as wonderful as I hoped it would be. But I don't think he's ready to hear that. So, I only tell him part of what I was thinking.

"That you regret it, regret me. That you're gonna get dressed and pretend this didn't happen between us. That you'll never look at me the same way again." His brown eyes wrinkle at the corners while I keep talking. "Dax, you just made me feel on top of the world. Please don't ruin this by regretting it." I turn my head to look at the ceiling above me now. The thought of him confirming my suspicions is so unbearable that I can't even bring myself to look at him. For all my confidence and teasing, I'm really worried he's about to destroy me.

The quiet envelopes us as we lay side by side, holding hands. The awkwardness of the situation is getting unbearable. As I prepare to stand up, the cold air from the open window sends shivers down my spine and causes goosebumps to appear on my skin, just as he says, "I don't regret it. How could I? Haven't stopped thinking about you ever since that kiss on Jake's birthday. You're phenomenal, inside and out. You exude sexiness and confidence. And you know what you want and you go get it. I'll never understand what you see in me," he huffs.

"Don't say that." Turning to look at him, I continue, "Do you realise how attractive you are, the way you present yourself? Dax, you're absolutely gorgeous. And when you talk about Jake, your eyes sparkle with pride and warmth, a reflection of the love and happiness you bring as a father. You've got it all. At least for me, you do." I smile. "Can we talk about it?" I ask.

"Yes, of course. But before anything else, let's get under the cover since your teeth are chattering again."

While I crawl under the blanket, Dax stands up to shut the window. I was expecting him to get dressed, but to my surprise, he crawls back into bed with me. Lying on our sides, we look into each other's eyes, feeling the warmth of our bodies next to each other. "Tell me what you're thinking, Dax," I say softly.

His gentle smile warms my heart as he tenderly pushes my curls away from my forehead. Blowing out a breath that warms my face, he murmurs, "Honestly, my biggest concern is Jake."

"Jake?"

"Yeah, I wouldn't want to cause any problems between the two of you, especially since you are so close. And I'm worried he'll hate me for it. For sleeping with you. I couldn't bear the idea of him being angry with either of us. He's all I have."

I wanna kiss him and snuggle up to his neck to make him feel better, but he didn't even kiss me during sex, so I don't wanna push it. However, I need to physically feel him, to have some form of touch. Reaching out, I gently place my hand on his cheek. "You're right. We *are* close. Jake is like a brother to me. He's supported me through some really hard times. He's important to me as well. If it wasn't for him, I might not be here. But I'll tell you a secret. I share everything with Jake. He's well-informed about my long-standing crush on you."

I observe the surprise in Dax's eyes as they widen.

"What?" he blurts.

"Mhm. I'm confident that he won't be mad at us because he knows how much I like you."

At least I hope he won't. For the past three years, he has patiently listened to me talk about his dad without ever mentioning that he was off-limits. Jake is a friend who loves me wholeheartedly. My biggest supporter. He is a constant reminder that bad days are part of life, but what matters is getting back up to enjoy the good days. He hopes I find my happy ending.

"There's a lot to unpack here, Tris." He rolls onto his back again, taking the covers with him.

"Hey, cover hogger. My butt is getting cold," I quip.

"Shit, sorry." Rolling back towards me, he tucks me back in.

"Look," I say. "We won't be going anywhere till the snow melts, so we have time to go over it all. That's if you want to, anyway. And just for the record, if you want to fuck me like that again, then I'm all for it."

Dax huffs out a laugh. "You're something else, you know that, Tris? Here's me having a crisis wanting to do the right thing and you still have my cock on your mind."

"So... is that a yes to the fucking?" I bat my eyelashes.

"Jesus. You should come with a warning label," he groans.

"Yeah? What would it say?" I know I'm fishing for compliments here, but I just can't help myself. I love teasing him.

"Trouble," he says, shaking his head.

"I'll wear it for you as long as I'm naked under it," I say playfully.

"See? Trouble with a capital T." His laugh makes me gooey inside. It's nice to see the lighter, fun side of him. I know we have lots to talk about, but I just hope he keeps an open mind about this thing between us. Because there is something here and I won't be told otherwise.

Dax looks serious again. "How about we take a nap, and when we wake up, I'll help you cook dinner, and we can talk then?" he suggests all teachery. I bet he's so hot in his classroom, standing up at the whiteboard, explaining 'there, their, and they're' to his students. "Are you okay? Are *we* okay?" He frowns.

"We're okay," I reassure him, a yawn catching me off guard. "You wanna be the big spoon or the little spoon?"

"How about neither? You stay on your side and I'll stay on mine." What a party pooper!

"Well, I'm a snuggler, if you haven't already gathered. So don't be surprised if you wake up covered in me." Dax smirks. "Let's just cuddle, spoon me, and if it slips in, it slips in, no biggie. You have my full consent, even if I'm sleeping." I give him a cheeky wink and turn over, backing up till my arse meets his body.

"You're impossible, you know that?" His arm wraps around my stomach, pulling me close till his hard meat is resting in my crack. This is what dreams are made of. I sigh and close my eyes. Sometimes dreams do come true.

Chapter Thirteen

"*Have yourself a merry little Christmas,*" I sing out loud. Michael Bublé is playing on my phone as I make us some food. And by food, I mean a charcuterie board. I'm no chef like Tris, but I can put cheese and crackers on a board. After I woke up from the best sleep of my life with Tris attached to me like a sloth, I realised we both went to sleep in a cum coma. I needed to have a shower. I tried not to wake Tris while I was getting up, but that was nearly impossible with him wrapped around me. And much to his disappointment, I did not '*slip my dick back in.*' I had a serious chat with myself and set new rules as the first ones went out the window. I've made up my mind not to do anything else with him until we've had a conversation about whatever this thing is between us.

Tris is currently in the bath that I prepared for him after my shower. I'm setting the table in the kitchen, and it looks good if I do say so myself. Next to the thick wedges of hard cheese were clusters of ripe red grapes, followed by a stack of crackers and a triangle of Summerset brie. The table was set with mature cheese, crackers, creamy garlic cheese, black olives, and fresh strawberries cut into pieces. I poured us each a couple of fingers of brandy from my pantry, the amber liquid glinting in the soft light. I felt like I would need something to take the edge off when I talked to Tris. My phone starts playing '*Santa Baby*' just as Tris comes walking into the kitchen.

My heart slams into my chest, bringing me to a full stop. The sight in front of me is... fucking temptation. Tris stands with a confidence that is both sexy and captivating. It leaves me speechless. I need to squish these spontaneous reactions quickly and remind myself he's a no-go area right now. I'm trying to shut down my body's response to him, but my mind is saying, '*fuck you, we want him*.' My rational brain clearly isn't strong enough to compete against Tris.

He comes strolling past me in the shortest shorts known to man. Surely, they are intended for a toddler. They're loose and red and look like they're made from the wings of fairies. The delicate material gently hugs his body in the perfect places without being too tight. Round flesh peeks out, taunting me with its perfect wiggle. His slim legs seem to go on for miles considering he's at least a foot shorter than my five-foot-eleven. The matching red crop top that leaves nothing to my imagination says, '*Teacher's Pet*.'

Fuck me all the way to Santa's workshop.

"What are those?" I say, nodding at his shorts. He looks around with absolutely no fucks given that my body is about two seconds from combusting at the sight of him.

"What are what?" he quips innocently.

"Them... things..." I mumble, pointing toward the offending flimsy material.

Looking down, he runs his hand down one side of his shorts, twisting slightly so the side so his plump cheek is on display... again.

"Oh, these are my lounge shorts. Do you like them?"

Yes, very much. Too much. I want to feel them rubbing across my face. How easy will the material tear in my hands?

I gulp. "They're a bit short. Maybe you want to put something else on. It can get cold in here." Jesus, could I sound any more like a dad?

He waves me off. "No, it's okay. I'll just whack some more wood on the fire if I get cold. I don't really like wearing much clothing," he shrugs. "I find it too restricting. I like to be able to bend and not get a wedgie. Look."

Jesus Christ, someone hold me back. As promised, he bends over right in front of me, exposing more of those fucking cheeks. Is it wrong that I want to scoop him up, lay him over my knees, and spank him for winding me up? *Yes, it's wrong. Very wrong. He's your son's best friend.*

Still bent over, he looks over his shoulder at me and bites his lip. I narrow my eyes. If I didn't know better, I would think he was doing it on purpose. Oh, what am I talking about? Of course, he's doing it on purpose. He can't bloody help himself. Oh, I'm so done for. He's a brat. I love brats. I turn and walk to the kitchen table, pick up my brandy, and gulp down the lot. I take a deep breath as the alcohol warms the back of my throat. I need to calm down before I follow through with my itching hands.

"Ooh, you made cheese and crackers! I brought all this stuff because Jake and Lewis normally come to my place over Christmas, and we stuff our faces. I'm trying not to break traditions even though they aren't here this year. Just *looove* stuffing my face... amongst other things, don't you?" he smacks his lips before picking up a grape and popping it in his mouth. "Have you heard from them?" He blinks innocently.

I pull out a chair for him to sit in and then I take the one opposite. "Yeah, Jake texted me this morning. Said they're going to a bistro today. They had a bit of snow, but nothing like here." Picking up a cracker, I spread some of the creamy garlic cheese and pass it to Tris. Then make one for myself.

"Thank you," he says, taking a bite. "Did you tell him you were here with me?"

Taking a bite of mine, I raise an eyebrow. "I didn't need to. You already told him."

A slight blush creeps up his neck. "Sorry. I only told him you'd come to help me and that you were snowed in. I didn't tell him about... us." He takes a small sip of his brandy and looks at me over the glass. "Is there an '*us*?'" Fuck, there's this vulnerable edge to his voice that makes me want to lay out the entire world at his feet.

Because I want there to be. An '*us*.' "I don't know, Tris," I mutter.

"Look, you know I like you? Like... *really* like you." I nod. Because yes, I know he does. "I'm pretty sure you like me, too, unless you go around sticking your dick in everyone you get snowed in with."

I spray my cracker all over the table, possibly snorting some crumbs out my nose too. Grabbing his glass, I take a sip to clear my mouth. For fuck's sake! This boy and his bluntness. He pops another grape into his mouth as he waits for my reply. I push my glasses back up my nose as I look at him. I have no defences around him. Taking a deep breath, I sigh, "Yes, to liking you. No, to the other part."

"That's what I thought. So... I'm thinking I'd really like to sample your cock again because, let me tell you, you know what you're doing with that weapon, and I very much would like it in me again." This time he eats a strawberry like he's just told me what the time is. Not a care in the world that he's offering me something I very much want. *Him.*

I'm a schoolteacher, so not much fazes me. But Tris. He seems to have the remote control to all my emotions. No one has ever been so upfront with me when it comes to sex. It's normally me asking the questions, but in a very demure way. Whereas Tris says it like it is and I'm actually really liking it. Why beat around the bush, as they say? It's refreshing. "What would this thing between us look like?"

"Well... we could just fuck while we're here. I mean, there's no TV, so it's kinda your fault that I need something to keep me occupied." The little shit smirks. My fingers start to itch again. I shake them out at my sides. "Once we leave here, we can part ways. Go back to our lives. It doesn't have to become a thing; I know you don't want me as a boyfriend, and I respect your boundaries. But we're both adults and horny and snowed in. Seems like the perfect combo to me," he winks. "Just think about it." He passes me a cracker with a wedge of cheese on.

My whole being is telling me he's perfect in every way. I don't do relationships, and he doesn't want one. We both love to have sex. We were on fire together. It's a win-win. Right?

We sit in a comfortable silence eating, with the Christmas songs in the background, mixed with the odd pop and crack of the fire. Once we're full, we clear away the food and I pour myself another drink.

"Let's go sit in the front room," I suggest as he follows me. Placing my drink down on the side table, I sit on the sofa. Tris comes and stands in front of me.

"Open up," he says, hands on his hips.

"What?" I frown, confused.

"Your arms. I want to sit too."

"Umm, you can sit here." I pat the space next to me.

"Nope, I'm sitting in your lap, big guy," he bites into his plump bottom lip, his gaze drifting to my groin.

Before I even have a chance to protest, his full weight is sitting on me. "Oof," I blurt. Both his arms go round my neck as he stretches out his legs on the sofa and gets comfy, rubbing on my dick that's popped up like a whack-a-mole. With one hand on his waist, I tentatively place the other on his leg to still him.

"See, this is much better. I told you I'm a snuggler." Resting his head on my shoulder, he makes a contented sigh.

We both stare into the fire, flames dancing around, and just like Tris, they're bright and full of energy, but deadly if not treated correctly. Can I really do this? Be with him just for now? The way he's settled so perfectly in my lap reminds me of how lonely I am by myself, even though it's my choice. Being around him makes me want more. More with him, at least.

"Okay," I say into his fragrant curls.

Sitting up, he looks at me with wide eyes, the fire reflected in them. "Okay?" He breathes.

"Yeah, checkmate. You win. We can be together. But just while we're here."

The squeal that comes out of him as he hugs me makes me laugh. God, he makes me feel alive.

Kissing my neck, he says, "You won't regret it. Just don't go falling in love with me, okay?"

Love? Me? Never gonna happen.

Chapter Fourteen

LOOKING OUT THE WINDOW at the blinding snow that the storm left behind, I can't quite believe the turn of events. The steam from my tea curls and swirls as I blow on it, the warm air tickling my nose before I take a sip. The moment Dax agreed with our plan, I felt an intoxicating surge of joy, like I was walking on clouds. Good things don't always come my way, so I'm determined to savour every precious moment I get to spend with him; right here, right now. I want to make the most of our time together and create memories that will linger long after we say goodbye—because we will inevitably go our separate ways.

When I suggested keeping this fling in the cabin, I meant it. At the time. But now I'm already worried about how I'm going to manage my everyday routines without his familiar presence. I had an incredible time last night. As soon as he gave his consent, I jumped into action, not wanting to lose a single second. I dropped to my knees in front of him and got my first proper look at his beaded cock.

It looked even more impressive up close, and he seemed happy with me exploring it. He was a panting mess by the time he came down my throat.

He made me stand, and, in one swift movement, tore my shorts from my body. My anger only lasted a second because once his warm mouth swallowed me down, all thoughts evaporated. He promised to replace them, and I intend to hold him to his word.

We'd spent the evening sharing stories and laughter by the warm glow of the fire, the initial passion we felt replaced by a deeper connection. Dax's eyes lit up as he described the joy of renovating the cabin, and he shared heartwarming stories of Jake growing up. How he met Jake's mother and how, through a shared understanding, they discovered they would never work as a couple, including his realisation that he was gay. He described his teaching job, his voice filled with amusement as he told stories about the kids that made me laugh until my stomach hurt. He explained how they have prank day at school each year, and how he always falls for their tricks.

As the last rays of sunlight faded, we built a crackling fire and walked hand in hand to the bedroom. The flickering flames in the living room cast a soft, warm glow through the doorway as he railed me for hours.

But when I woke this morning, a feeling of change had settled over me, like a shift in the very air I breathed. I felt a loneliness I had never experienced before. I realised I wasn't just looking for casual sex anymore; I wanted something deeper. I crave the comfort of waking up to the warmth of a loved one, their breath soft against my skin. I'm looking for someone to share my hopes and dreams with. To cook meals for, to shower with love and affection, to spoil rotten, and to let myself be spoiled, too. Maybe it's my subconscious playing tricks on me because I know Dax isn't interested in anything more. Why do you always crave the things that are just out of reach?

After getting up, I took a quick shower, cleaned the kitchen, and made some croissants. Two of the delicious pastries may have accidentally found their way into my mouth. To keep the soft fruit from spoiling, I tossed together a colourful fruit salad, saving it for later.

Since it's lunchtime and Dax hasn't woken up yet, I decide to open one of my presents from under the tree. Today's gift is a super-snug gingerbread bodycon romper that fits me like a glove.

Just as I finish my tea, the warm mug still lingering in my hands, strong, warm arms slide around my waist, followed by a gentle kiss on my neck. No hesitation. It just feels right, like it's supposed to be. My lips are tingling for another kiss, but I know I need to be patient and wait for Dax to be ready. The last thing I want to do is make him run, not after I've gone to all this trouble to get him. Almost.

"Morning," he says, his voice raspy with sleep.

"You mean afternoon?" I joke.

A low chuckle rumbles in his chest. "Yeah, sorry about that. I can't remember the last time I slept in so late. I'm usually up with the birds!"

I turn my head slightly, and our eyes meet. "Maybe it's because you worked hard last night," a cheeky smile plays on my lips.

He smirks. "Yeah maybe."

I turn back to looking outside, placing my cup on the windowsill, loving the way he's holding me. My hands clasped around his arms, the gentle sway of our bodies soothing me. I let out a deep sigh. I'm desperate to hold on to this feeling, this moment, for just a little while longer.

"What's wrong?" he asks, his voice low, laced with concern.

Everything. Nothing. All of it. "I don't know."

My stomach chooses this moment to growl. "You hungry? Have you eaten? Want me to make you something?" he says.

I haven't eaten in a while. Maybe he's right. Maybe I'm just hangry. I'll feel better once I get some food. "Sure, I'll take a sandwich."

"A sandwich? You sure? I can probably make some pasta."

"Dax, don't underestimate the power of a sandwich. It's like food from the gods!"

The warmth of his breath sends shivers down my spine as his laughter ruffles my curls. "All right, tell me what you want in it?"

"Hmm... banana, sugar, and lots of real butter. You can't have a sarnie with fake shit!"

"But real butter is so hard, it'll tear the bread."

"Dax, Dax, Dax," I say, turning to him and shaking my head. "You never know when a sandwich emergency might pop up, so I'm always prepared! There's a plate of butter on the side."

My hands cup his face. I feel the rough stubble of his unshaven cheeks against my palms. He looks even more handsome and rugged than when he was clean-shaven. "You've got a lot to learn from me." He blushes adorably.

I let go of his face before I lean in and place a kiss on his lips. Stepping aside, I start to make my way to the kitchen. His hand closes around my wrist, his fingers warm against my skin. "Hold on, let me take a look at what you're wearing."

He twirls me around, groaning with approval, the sound making my chest flutter with happiness.

"Come on, a delicious sandwich waits for no man!" I tell him.

I give Dax a little sandwich-making lesson, showing him exactly how I like it, just in case he needs to know for future reference. You can only hope, right? Dax makes himself a ham and cheese sandwich, and I grab a bowl of crisps for us to share. We sit down at the table to eat.

"So," he says, his voice muffled by the bread in his mouth. "I feel like I dominated the conversation last night, talking mostly about myself. I didn't even ask you anything about your life. So... tell me about you."

"Not much to tell, really," I mutter, swallowing the last bit of my sandwich. "Jake probably told you all about me."

Wrinkles crease his forehead. "To be honest, Jake is really protective of you, and he doesn't tell me much."

That makes me wonder if he's asked about me before. The thought of Jake not mentioning me, fills me with a mix of love and a tinge of sadness. While I appreciate Jake keeping my business private, I can't help but feel a little disappointed he didn't mention me at all to his dad.

"Hey, I see that look in your eyes. Please don't take it personally," he says, voice softening. "Jake was just being a good friend to you.

Really, it was none of my business. But if it makes you feel any better, I ask him about you every week during our FaceTime calls."

"You do?" I exclaim, raising an eyebrow in disbelief.

"Yep, he always tells me I should just ask you myself, but it feels awkward to call you out of the blue."

"I mean, you absolutely could have. I had no idea you had my number."

A blush creeps onto Dax's cheeks as he pops a few crisps into his mouth. "Yeah, well, it wasn't easy to get, trust me," he grumbles, a scowl etched on his face.

"You actually ask about me every week, huh?" My stupid heart leaps in my chest, a foolish little dance. I tell myself it's nothing, but I can't shake the feeling that he's more than just curious about who his son hangs out with. Why else would he want to know?

"Not gonna live that down, am I?" I shake my head at him. "Anyway, stop avoiding the question. Give me something, anything. I'm curious to learn more about Tristan Hayes."

Now, there's a million-dollar question. Who is Tristan Hayes? "Well, I'm just me." I shrug. "Good friend of your son, a university dropout. A guy who lives alone. I don't even have a cat," I joke.

His head tilts to the side, the silent gesture a clear signal that he's not buying my bullshit. I've never really been comfortable talking about myself—I always feel like I'm being judged, and my flaws are all I can see. I blow out a breath, running my fingers through my tangled curls before sinking back into my chair and meeting the intense gaze of his deep brown eyes staring back at me.

"I work at a homeless shelter. We're a halfway house for folks who are struggling with addiction and living on the streets. We provide meals twice a day, along with basic care. It's a safe space offering a few hours of comfort and nurturing. And I absolutely love it."

"How did you come to work there?" he asks, sounding genuinely interested.

"University wasn't the right fit for me. The workload with its deadlines was too stressful. I could see that Jake was happy and flourishing in his new environment, but I felt out of place and was struggling. On my way home from a night out, a kebab in hand, I stumbled over a guy curled up under a duvet on the pavement. Instead of letting me fall, he reached out and caught me. He was an elderly gentleman, his eyes shining with kindness beneath the dirt. Maybe it was silly, but I sat down next to him and gave him my meal. He explained that he'd become homeless after his business failed and his marriage ended. As I walked home, I was reminded of the fragility of life—how everything we hold dear can disappear in the blink of an eye. I left school the next day and went to the nearby shelter to offer my help. I haven't regretted it for a second." I smile.

"That's incredible, Tristan!" He reaches out and opens his palm, beckoning me to place my hand on top of his. "You are truly amazing, and I can only imagine how thrilled that guy must have been to meet you."

"His name is Sam, short for Samuel. He goes to the shelter. When I'm on food duty, I always stash away some extra bread rolls and little packets of real butter for him to take with him when he leaves."

Dax snorts with laughter. "Of course you do. You have such a big heart filled with empathy for everyone around you. What about your family? Are you close to them? Mum? Dad? Siblings?"

Ugh, here comes the dreaded moment of telling him about Mum. I love talking about her, don't get me wrong, but I don't want Dax to think I'm playing the victim. People always assume you're hard done by when you have a sick parent, and I don't want to come across that way. His pity is the last thing I need.

"Nope, I never knew my dad. I don't have any siblings, and my mum is living with dementia. She's in a nursing home full-time, and I visit her every week, bringing her fresh flowers and a smile. So, it's just me." I give him a fake smile and get up, taking my plate with me to the sink, waiting for the usual, '*Oh, I'm so sorry, Tris. It must be so hard. You're a saint. I don't know how you cope.*'

A heavy silence hangs in the air, and his words don't come. Slowly, I turn around, my gaze meeting Dax's as he remains seated at the table. His arms, thick and strong, are crossed over his chest, and as he looks me up and down, a blush rises on my cheeks. "Did I say you could get up from the table?" he growls, the sound making my stomach clench. I bite my lower lip and shake my head.

"That's what I thought." He stands up so abruptly that his chair topples over with a loud thump. He clears the table in an instant, sweeping his hand across it and sending everything tumbling to the floor with a deafening crash. "You. Here. Now."

Of course, I fucking obey. I'm not stupid. He heaves me up and, with a slight grunt, settles me on the table. "I wasn't finished eating."

Pinned beneath the weight of his hand as he pushes me back, I stare up at the rough-hewn beams above as the fabric of my bodysuit tears. Fucking hell, I'll have no clothes left at this rate... "*Oooooh!*" His warm tongue meets my hole. I'll just zip my lips. I'll play the role of his gingerbread man. Eat me.

Tris 3 Dax 100.

Chapter Fifteen

WHEN TRIS TALKED ABOUT his work, his face glowed with a passion that was contagious. I could tell how much joy his job brought him. It was like he radiated light. And the way he tried to wave off his mother's dementia, like he thought I was going to judge him for it or offer some trite platitudes. His demeanour, the way he held himself and looked at me, suggested he was used to people's sympathy and pity. Kind words, spoken with sincerity, were meaningless to him, as he'd heard them countless times before.

Did I want to be one of those people? To be the one he could turn to, the one who would be there for him, offering comfort and understanding? Did I want to wrap him up in cotton wool and protect him from the world? Abso-fucking-lutley I did. But that was not what he needed at this moment in time. Tris is a strong man who doesn't need another person to barge into his life and tell him he's a great guy. He knows that already. Tris needs someone to show him how incredible he can feel, to be treated like royalty. Like my little fox. Right now, he needs a reminder that he's more than just his work or his role as a dutiful son. And I am damn well going to do that for him.

I'm going to gorge myself on this man until his words become just a jumbled mess of unintelligible noises.

Righting my overturned chair, I placed it back in front of him, ensuring I had the best seat in the house. Sitting down, I'm greeted with the perfectly formed ring of muscle, pink and ripe, practically screaming at me to devour it.

And devour I will.

I tuck myself in closer to the table so I can feast on him. I indulge in him like my favourite meal, licking at his rosy rim with the tip of my tongue, teasing the tightness. Once he softens beneath me, I suck his pucker into my mouth, eliciting a string of curses from him. He's starting to open up for me, letting me in, and when his hole unclenches beneath my tongue, I shove it inside him, his heat welcoming me. I circle my tongue around inside him and he moves with me, his hips lifting to meet my thrusts. I'm tempted to let him come on my tongue like this, swallowing down his orgasm. Reeling myself in, though, I add my fingers to the mix, stretching him to the point where three of my thick fingers can fit inside comfortably. His withering grumbles are music to my ears—it means I'm doing my job right. I prepare him so that he's nice and supple and will withstand the fury of the hard thrusts I'm soon to give him. The ones where you have nothing else on your mind but simply claiming a beautiful body. I have to mould his hole to my cock. So that it remembers me. Even when he's doing the most mundane things, like walking home or doing his food shopping, I want the thought of us to play on a loop in his mind. I want my DNA interwoven with his, a tangible connection to him even when we're apart.

"Please Dax," he begs, his voice trembling.

His legs are so relaxed, almost boneless at my touch, that he can barely keep them on the table. I grant him a moment's reprieve from my relentless assault. Standing, I tear the remaining fabric from his body. He's bared and helpless, completely at my mercy. His usually pale skin is flushed pink, and the freckles that dust his body like a scattering of stars make me want to count every single one. Taste them. Name them all. This boy has me completely captivated. I can't think straight.

"I need you," he whispers, panting. The lust in his veins turns his blue eyes almost black, yet there is a tenderness in his gaze, a trust that makes my heart ache with a strange vulnerability. No one I've ever been with has made me feel so incredibly, profoundly powerful and weak at the same time. Tris's complete submission to me, surrendering his body, is utterly extraordinary.

My hands reach for him, and grasping them, I pull him up. "Come with me."

The fireplace crackles and hisses, warming the room as I lead him to it. "Let me get rid of these clothes," I tell him. "Stand right there, don't move," I instruct. "And watch me."

Slowly, I pull off my black soft-knit jumper, letting the material glide up over my skin, and toss it carelessly onto the sofa. Tris watches me like the good boy he is, his knuckles white as he clenches his fists, almost as if he's holding back a primal urge to attack. My lips curve into a smirk, enjoying his reaction as he furrows his brow in a deep frown. With a gentle tug, I release the button on my black slacks and feel the fabric fall into a pile around my ankles.

The gasp from Tris is exactly what I wanted, a perfect reaction to the unexpected.

"You went commando." He tilts his head to one side, his clenched fist pressed against his chest, as though his heart might burst from its confines.

I smirk. "I wanted to surprise you."

"Oh, you did," he says, a mischievous glint in his eye. "Naked looks good on you."

"Believe me, little fox, it suits you much better."

Stepping out my slacks, I bend over to remove my socks, making us both equal in our nakedness.

"Now... I'm going to get on my knees for you. I'm going to suck you and tease you till you come in my mouth. Then I want you on all fours. Right here on this rug with that sweet arse pointing upwards. You hear me?"

"Yes, Dax. I hear you... sir."

Oh, he's back to being a brat. His excitement leaves a wet trail on his stomach. "I'm going to use your cum to fuck you." Tris gasps and his eyes reach his brows, mouth hanging open. "Got it?" I ask.

Nodding, he replies, "Anything you want, Dax." His voice comes out clipped. "Please, I don't want to wait no more. Please do all the dirty things to me." There's my desperate little fox.

"Come here." Stepping forward, his arms wrap around my neck, skin to skin. His hard, wet cock presses into my thigh as I grasp each globe.

I'm drowning in the desire to kiss him, but something is keeping me from doing it. I untangle his arms from around my neck and drop to my knees, the intoxicating scent of his arousal swirling around me. As his thighs quiver, I rub my face against them, feeling the hardness of his shaft and the softness of his neatly trimmed auburn hair, marking myself in his smell. Leaning back, I look at him. Greeting me is a cock that is perfectly in proportion, with a subtle lean to the left. I run my tongue along the beautiful blue vein before playfully flicking the tip of his cockhead. Hands seize my head, holding me firmly in place.

With gentle sucks, his swollen head presses against my tongue as I guide him deep into the back of my throat.

"*Fuuuuck*, that feels so good. Don't stop," he begs.

So I don't. Even though his grip on my hair is so tight it makes my scalp ache, I keep going. It fuels my determination. I don't resist as he takes control, using my face for his own pleasure.

"I'm close, fuck. So... good. Yeah, just like that," he moans.

Inserting two fingers into his loosened hole, I curl them and press down, savouring the warm spurts that fill my mouth as his orgasm peaks.

"Your mouth," he gasps. "*Aggghhhhh*. Lord, love a duck."

I want to laugh at him, but I can't risk spilling any of his precious milk. The urge to swallow him down, to make him a part of me, is almost overwhelming. Eager to get going, I tap his leg. He drops to all fours, his arms outstretched in front of his face, and he nuzzles his nose into the fuzzy rug. I widen his legs and spread his cheeks, feeling his cum drip from my mouth and glide down over his opening. With a gentle push, I insert my finger into him, depositing cum inside. Then I drop some onto my own desperately hard cock, ensuring that every inch is covered. With one foot planted on the floor and the other leg bent at the knee, I grip his hips tightly and thrust hard into him.

"*Fuuuck*," I say, and we both groan simultaneously. "Such a fucking good hole. Who do you belong to?"

"You," he whispers, his voice barely audible. "You have me completely, Dax," he declares.

That's right. I do. My primal instincts kick in, and I dominate him with intense and rapid movements, pounding into him until sweat drenches my body. Until I can no longer ignore the buzzing, almost electric sensation in my lower back. I feel a rush of heat as I release inside him, my body trembling with pleasure. I stay there until my body settles down, hugging him tightly with my cock.

As I slide out, I see his asshole clenching, and then our combined release starts dribbling out, compelling me to taste it. Lowering myself, I use my tongue to scoop up the deliciousness and send it down my throat. Fuck me. Can one become addicted to cum? Asking for a friend.

"What are to doing?" Tris rasps, his body still panting from the exertion. Scooping up some more, I lean over his sweaty back and allow it to slide off my tongue onto his lips. "Fuck, is that us?"

"Mhm, don't you just love the way we taste?"

"Dax, that's disgustingly dirty... we taste delicious. Give me more." Spreading his cheeks, allowing more of the sweet, sticky liquid to flow out, I sample some before giving the rest to him. Then I collapse next to him, my hand gently tracing patterns on his back, until goosebumps appear. I don't know how I'm meant to give him up. He doesn't belong to me, but it doesn't matter how much I tell myself that this will end. Even though my brain knows it, my heart refuses to listen. I want him more than ever.

Chapter Sixteen

"Hey, Dax! Get your cute little tush over here and baste this turkey."

It's not actually a turkey. It's a chicken. When I picked up food for this week, I knew I'd be here for Christmas, but a whole-ass turkey would have been wasted on me. "Here you go," I say, passing him the baster, which looks like a massive pipette.

"What exactly am I doing?" he inquires.

"Basting. It's tradition."

With one eyebrow shooting up, he gives me a look that suggests I'm out of my mind. "I've never heard of basting a chicken as a tradition. I always thought it was the Christmas cake you stirred and made a wish on."

"Eh, semantics." I shrug. "Mum and I didn't always have a lot of money to buy ingredients for a cake, so we made the best of what we had. A Christmas baste became our tradition. So, squirt."

"Yes, sir," he chuckles, shaking his head.

"Hey, that's my line!" I give Dax a playful pat on the backside as I fill the pot with water for the potatoes he has just peeled. It's hard to believe Christmas is already here—the excitement of the day ahead bubbles inside me. I woke up, unable to contain my joy, jumping up and down on the bed—much to Dax's annoyance. The blow job I gave him more than made up for it, though.

"So, what's up next, Chef?"

Dax's voice is close to my ear as he leans over my shoulder, his hands on my hips, sending shivers shooting down my spine. He's doing this more and more now, touching and staying close to me. And although he hasn't kissed me yet, I'm enjoying every second spent with him.

"Well, there's not much we can do right now. The vegetables are prepped and ready, the chicken is cooking in the oven, and I just need to put these potatoes on to boil. Then I thought we could just relax for a bit."

Dax's phone buzzes. He pulls it out of his pocket, checks the message, then smirks.

"What?" I ask, curious.

"Jake just texted; he wants to FaceTime." Dax smiles adorably.

"He does?" I really miss my friend. I'm so glad he's finally taking some time for himself, and we text almost every day. But I miss hanging out with him. "Cool, let's sit down at the table."

Dax sets his phone down by the fruit bowl and sits next to me.

"Do I look all right?" I ask him.

"You look very... edible!" he says, licking his lips and tackling me, tickling me so hard I can't stop laughing and almost fall off the chair. He just manages to grab me by my skirt and pull me back in place. Dax unwrapped today's gift, revealing a short red pleated skirt, red-and-white striped stockings, and a sheer silver long-sleeved crop top.

"*Stoooop*," I laugh, batting his hands away. Just then, his phone rings. We compose ourselves, and Dax answers the call, clearing his throat as he sends me a quiet warning with his eyes.

Jake and Lewis beam at the camera, filling the screen with their infectious smiles.

"Merry Christmas, Dad! Merry Christmas, Tris! Dang, Tristan, you look smoking hot. I can't believe you're still single!" Jake chirps.

I blush furiously and give him a look that could kill because he knows I'm head over heels for the man sitting right next to me. His smile is the mirror image of his father's, both holding the same mischievous twinkle in their eyes.

"Merry Christmas, son. Lewis. To what do we owe the honour of this call?"

"What? I need an excuse to call my dad and best friend on Christmas Day?" Jake says, a mock-offended look on his face.

"Course not." Dax settles back in the chair, a knowing smirk playing on his lips.

"Well..." Jake says, drawing out the word, leaving a lingering hint of intrigue in the air. "Seeing as you asked... Look!"

Jake's hand, adorned with a gleaming gold band, shoots out towards the screen.

"No fucking way!" I shout, getting closer to the phone. "You're engaged! Oh my God, Jake. When? How? Give me all the details."

Jake's laughter fills the entire cabin. "Lewis surprised me last night by taking me to see the Eiffel Tower all lit up. It was so romantic, and then he got down on one knee and asked, didn't you, babe?" He leans down and gives Lewis a quick, gentle kiss on the lips.

"Lewis, you sneaky devil. You kept that quiet," I tease.

"Sorry, Tris. You know I love you, but you and Jake talk about *everything*." Hmm, not exactly *everything*. But it's fair. "I didn't want to risk ruining the surprise, so I kept my plans a secret. I wanted it to be perfect for Jake. Forgive me?"

Lewis gives me those big, pleading puppy eyes. In fact, they both have them. Stupid love-hearts-shooting-out-their-arse looks on their faces. I realise I want that. I'm not jealous of my friends, but I'm sad that I might never get to look the way they do.

Happy. Content. *In love.*

"I can't be mad when you've made my best friend look like *Dopey*." A smile stretches across my face. "I'm so happy for you both! Congratulations!"

"Thank you, Tris," Jake says, smiling. "I wanted to make sure you and Dad were the first to find out. Although you've been pretty quiet, Dad?"

I watch Dax, a wide grin still plastered across his face, as he stares at the screen.

"You were in on this, weren't you?" I ask him.

Turning his head slowly, he gives me a mischievous look, wiggling his eyebrows before returning his attention to Jake. "Yeah, I knew already."

"What?" Jake screeches. He turned to his fiancé, who looks a little sheepish.

"Yeah, I, um... asked your dad if it was okay," Lewis croaks.

Jake and I both sigh in contentment, the sound of *ahhhs* escaping our lips. If that isn't the cutest fucking thing ever. My heart melts at the sight of them, their sweetness filling me with warmth. Watching them kiss and hug, tears well up in my eyes, blurring my vision. Turning to Dax, I offer him a warm smile. My hand rests on my chest, right over my heart. The big softie gives me a smile that warms me from the inside out, the most sincere and genuine one I've ever seen from him. He beams with pride, his heart overflowing with joy for his son. He really is a great dad to Jake.

"Okay, okay. Let's keep this PG around me, yeah?" We all laugh. Dax's big hand squeezes my leg, a silent gesture of comfort, as I wipe my tears with a napkin. "Seriously, though. I'm so happy for both of you. I have full confidence that Lewis will take good care of you. That's the one thing I've always wanted for you, Jake. To be happy."

"I am, Dad. You and Mom have taught me so much about what to look for in a partner and how to chase my dreams. I appreciate the sacrifices you've both made for me."

"Always, son," Dax declares.

"Tristan," Jake continues. "You're the best friend anyone could ask for," he says with a grin, "and I'd be so proud to have you stand by my side as my best man."

Cue ugly crying. Dax gives in and wraps his arms around me, offering comfort as I cry into his shirt. I could have sworn I felt his lips brush a gentle kiss against my head.

He passes me a fresh napkin from the stack on the table as I wipe myself clean.

With a shaky voice, I turn back to the phone. "Yes. I'd be honoured to be your best man."

"Thank heavens, I was afraid I had upset you with all that snot you just dripped on Dad's shirt."

"Fuck you, asshole! It's not every day you find out your bestie got engaged."

Dax's hand returns to my leg, a low chuckle rumbling in his chest as he looks at me with amusement.

"Now, now, children," Dax jokes. "Jake and Lewis, we're absolutely ecstatic for you both! We couldn't be more thrilled! Are we still on to celebrate New Year's at my place?" he asks his son and future son-in-law.

"I spoke to Mum last night, and she mentioned she's staying with her friend, who just went through a breakup. She said she'd message you. So, it's just going to be Lewis and me."

"Okay, sounds good. We can catch up then. We'll let you go," Dax says. "Tris is whipping up a delicious dinner, and the smells coming from the kitchen are making my mouth water."

He squeezes my leg, his touch firm and reassuring. God, I hate that I can't share my happiness with Jake. I want to shout it from the rooftops to show him just how amazing Dax is. How good we are together. But that's never going to happen. I push those thoughts to the back of my mind, trying to be present and in the moment.

I plaster a smile onto my face, watching my friend's infectious joy, and desperately choke back the bitter tears threatening to spill, pretending they are tears of happiness for them, not tears of sorrow for myself.

"Tris will take good care of you," Jake says, winking.

"Oh, I know," Dax replies, his voice quiet and thoughtful.

I have to shut this down quickly before I end up confessing everything to Jake. "Congrats again to you both! Merry Christmas, Jake! I hope it's the best one yet, and I can't wait to hear all about it when we see each other." I blow a kiss in his direction, and he pretends to grab it and puts it over his heart.

"Bye, kids," Dax says. "Remember, don't do anything I wouldn't do. And if you do, be safe."

A hearty laugh escapes his lips while we all groan in response. I silently mouth, *Love you, bye* to Jake before ending the call.

"Wow," I say, exhaling slowly and relaxing back into the chair. "I can't believe it. Jake is actually getting married!"

"Pretty cool, huh? Hopefully, they'll give me grandkids one day."

Kids. '*I want them, too,*' I want to scream. I'm ready for a family. I want to create new traditions with the people around me while sharing the old ones that are important to me. My heart yearns to be a parent, raise tiny humans, and fill a home with love and laughter. I want the whole shebang.

The older I get, the more I fear that my happily ever after is a fading dream, a distant hope that may never come true. I'm only twenty-four, so people say I have my whole life ahead of me, but the thought of being alone forever keeps me up at night. It feels like a constant ache, a nagging fear that whispers I'll always be lonely. Jake will now be lost in his love bubble, as he deserves. And once Dax leaves the cabin, he will probably move on with his life, not giving me another thought. I'll be on my own again.

"You ever wish you'd had more kids?" I blurt before realising it.

Dax frowns, looking at me in thought. "Yeah, maybe. I mean, there was a time when I really wanted a sibling for Jake..." he hesitates. "But then, I guess life had other plans for me." The look in his eyes is indecipherable, but his voice sounds sad. Then he seems to shake himself. "Doesn't matter now, anyway. Too late at my age." He smiles at me, and I just want to jump into his lap, screaming, '*No, no, it's not! It's not too late! I'll give you all the babies you want*!' But obviously, I don't. I'm not desperate. Yeah, right. Who am I kidding?

"I'm going to go chop some wood outside. You okay in here?" Dax says, getting up and grabbing his axe by the door. "Is there anything you need me to do?" His question hangs in the air, oblivious to the silent battle going on in my mind. The '*Breed me, Dax*!' gets stuck in the back of my throat, thankfully.

Turning towards him, I force on a broad smile. "I've got everything under control in here for now," I assure him. "You go out and do manly things in the freezing cold."

He chuckles, a soft, throaty sound that fills the air. "All right. Give me a shout if you need anything."

'*I need YOU,*' my heart screams in my chest, but all I can do is nod silently. The door closes behind him with a soft click, leaving me alone in the room. I sink into the soft cushions of the sofa, letting out a quiet sob, indulging in a pity party for one.

Chapter Seventeen

THE DINNER TRIS COOKED for us was absolutely delicious. If I'd been home as I originally planned, I would have simply made a microwave meal. It wouldn't have been worth the effort to cook a fancy dinner just for myself. I ate until I couldn't possibly fit in another bite—even if someone paid me!

But something is not right with Tristan. He didn't say much during dinner and was silent as we bustled around, wrapping up the remaining food. The clatter of dishes was a stark contrast to his stillness. Ever since Jake called, he's seemed a bit off, like something is weighing heavily on his mind. Tris's usual playful demeanour is gone, replaced by a withdrawn and subdued silence.

For the past hour, I've been lying on the couch, listening to him clean and mutter to himself as if he's the only one in the room. The cabin is now sparkling clean, almost unnaturally so, and it makes me wonder if he's trying to avoid me.

Turning my head from where I'm lying on my back, I see Tris attempting to lift the basket near the fireplace, which I had already loaded with firewood.

"Whatcha doin'?" I ask in a gentle tone, afraid that a louder voice might make him jump.

"Oh... um... I was just gonna... get some more... you know... wood," he mumbles, avoiding my gaze.

Yep, there's definitely something wrong. I shift onto my side, propping my head on my hand, and study him. "It's full. You can't get any more in there."

He squints at the basket, his brow furrowed in displeasure, before letting it go. "Yeah... Okay. You're right. I'll check if the bathroom needs cleaning."

Just as he turns, I grab his hand, stopping him in his tracks. "Is everything okay?" I glance up at him. He looks adorable in a red-and-white candy cane short set, the stripes making him look like a little piece of holiday cheer.

With his eyes downcast, he refuses to look at me. "Yeah, I'm good."

Not sure who he's trying to kid, I counter, "If you're so great, why won't you look at me?"

Those blue eyes, so sad, look at me then. "See?" He fakes a smile, trying to appear cheerful. "I'm fine."

His hand tugs against mine, but I hold him tight, refusing to let go. Not so fast.

"Tristan," I say, raising an eyebrow in challenge.

A heavy sigh escapes his lips, his shoulders slumping as he casts his gaze back down at the floor.

"Come here." I pull my hand away from my head and pat the sofa. "Lie down with me."

His hesitation makes me worry even more because *my* Tristan would have eagerly jumped at the chance to be close to me. *My Tristan*. While he's not *technically* anything to me, I'm beginning to entertain the idea of wanting him to become something more.

He sighs and lies down with his body facing mine; a silent truce reached. I pull him closer, our bodies pressed tightly together, as I intertwine my leg with his to keep him close. With my free hand, I rub gentle circles on his back, inhaling the warm, comforting scent of his skin. The orange-scented shampoo wafts up from his hair and envelops me as he presses his face into my chest. His curls brush against my face, getting caught in the rough, prickly stubble that has grown since I've been here.

After a few minutes, his body relaxes, and the tension that had been knotting his shoulders melts away. My fingers move slowly up and down his back, easing him until his breathing calms.

"What's going on?" I ask carefully. "And don't say nothing."

His hand tightens around my shirt, and he takes a deep breath. "Was it Jake? Are you upset that he's getting married?"

Pulling his head back to look at me, he furrows his brow, creating deep creases in his forehead. "What? *No*! Jake getting married is the absolute best news! It's just..." He lets out another long, weary sigh. "It's stupid, really."

"Nothing you say is stupid. Tell me."

"I just... I just want the same thing Jake and Lewis have, that's all," he says, his voice tight with longing. "I'm lonely."

My heart breaks into a thousand pieces. The impact of those two words is so forceful that it feels like someone has punched me in the chest, knocking the air out of my lungs. Tristan is lonely. I realise now that my knowledge of him has been limited to the brief, cheerful interactions I've witnessed during phone calls with Jake. He always came across as energetic and carefree.

Being with him in such close confines, I've come to see that Tris has many sides: the caring side, the empathetic side, the kind, generous, and loving side, and the side that shows he has an honest heart. Then there's the unsure, unworthy side to him, the one that whispers doubts in his ear, the one that makes him second guess himself. Then comes the mischievous side. A man who is fiery and sexy, assertive yet submissive. *A brat*. But I never thought he'd be lonely.

The realisation strikes me with a jolt. I wasn't just fond of my little fox; I was genuinely starting to care for him. Every part of him.

"Lonely? What do you mean? You've got Jake and Lewis. Your mum. I'm certain you have coworkers who appreciate your hard work, and I'm positive the visitors to the shelter adore you." *And you have me.*

"You're right. I do have all that, and during the day when I'm busy, that's enough. But then, at night, I go home to an empty flat, and the silence is deafening. No one to ask me about my day. No one to cook for. No one to cuddle. Not since Mum..." He stops talking.

I didn't realise what I was saying when I mentioned his mum. Even though my mother has a tendency to meddle, I'm fortunate to still have her around. I can't fathom the emotional turmoil of having a mother physically present but mentally absent. My fingers dig deeper into his back as I squeeze him tighter.

"I just want someone to love me." His soft, whispered words pierce my heart. "Spending time with you has shown me I crave something more meaningful than just random hookups. I want a relationship that's full of depth, one that will make me laugh, cry, and grow. I want to go on dates and feel the romance of making love to my partner on a rainy night with the window open. Lazy nights on the sofa, with a warm blanket and a bowl of popcorn, watching films and dreaming about our future. I'm afraid I'll have none of that."

He sniffs, his tears leaving damp patches on my shirt, "So yeah, Jake's news upset me a little, but not in the way you think," he whispers.

Tris wants everything I consciously make an effort to avoid. I enjoy meeting people through apps and having fun dates. If we end up back at their place or a hotel, I always make it clear I'm not looking for anything serious. The idea of a relationship has never held any appeal for me. But a little voice inside me, like a persistent itch, keeps whispering that Tris is the one who could change everything.

My heart races at the way he's looking at me. We're so close. "I've not kissed anyone since Jake's birthday three years ago," I confess. Wide-eyed, he looks at me but says nothing. "I... everyone else just... wasn't you." His breath hitches. "What are you doing to me, Tris?"

Everything goes quiet; the crackling fire, the wind outside, and my breath. They're all suspended in a moment of perfect bliss, almost as if the world has stopped to celebrate this perfect moment. Our lips meet again. My stomach lurches, and a rush of warmth and excitement floods my body like butterflies taking flight. It's like everything has come full circle; the missing piece of my heart has finally been found. My hand finds the nape of his neck and my fingers trace the curve of his skin as he opens for me.

His taste is even better than I remembered, a perfect blend of sweetness and something uniquely him, a taste that lingers on my tongue. I reclaim his mouth, our tongues intertwining in a passionate dance. A whimpering sound vibrates in my mouth. I can't tell if it's coming from me or him. We kiss slowly, lingering on each other's lips, the passion building until it explodes, desperate and hungry. Then, we pull back, the fire still burning, and resume our slow, sensual dance. Even though we are both clearly aroused, our deep connection keeps us from doing anything more than enjoying the intoxicating kiss.

The hours melt away as we lie there, our lips swollen and pulsing, the warmth of our bodies pressed together, our hands intertwined in each other's hair, gentle fingers tracing soft strands. Both our cocks softened, knowing that we would not be taking this any further.

We lie there, our lips brushing, taking precious moments to catch our breath, but the pull of the kiss is too strong, and soon we're lost in it again. It's like a sweet nectar for our souls, a taste we can't get enough of. Feeding off each other into the night. I realise, with unwavering certainty, that I won't be able to give Tristan up. I belong to him, and he belongs to me. All my preconceived notions about commitment go out the window. I plan to confess my feelings to him in the morning, and I really hope he feels the same. Something tells me he does. He has to. When he confessed he was lonely and wanted someone special in his life, I got the distinct feeling he was talking about me.

Please, let him be talking about me.

Chapter Eighteen

Opening the door to my flat, I watched as my mail slid across the floor. The sweet, artificial scent of the Christmas berries' air freshener clashes with a pungent, rancid odour that assaults my nostrils. My bags hit the floor with a thud as I dump them, and I go straight to find the culprit. Following the rotten smell through the living room, to the kitchen, I see the fridge door is slightly ajar. Crap, I must not have closed it properly in my haste to leave. Pulling open the fridge, I nearly gag.

Brie.

I was too heartbroken to even eat at the services on the drive home, so luckily, I have nothing to throw up. Using kitchen tongs, I pick up the fluffy cheese and throw it away. I quickly tie up the bag and take it outside to the bins.

Standing in my living room following *CheeseGate*, I take in the dusty bookshelves, the worn cream rug, and the faded white wallpaper which all remain the same, but in me, everything feels different.

My body gives way to my emotions, and I sink into the deep green cushions of my sofa, letting out a heavy sigh. I think I might have fucked up. I feel terrible, but I had to do what was best for me and try to protect my mental health. My heart sinks in my chest. I knew what was coming. I knew how this would end. Dax was going to tell me that our 'fun' had reached its end and that he didn't want anything serious. I couldn't bear the pain of hearing him say those words out loud.

So, I left.

A cunty move, sure. I took the coward's way out. And I feel shitty about it.

Waking in his arms as the first rays of dawn kissed the sky, I heard a faint sound that sent dread to my core. Rain. Drumming a steady rhythm on the windows, it was like the sound of doom, telling me the snow had melted. It was time to leave. To leave behind the bubble we'd created where we briefly allowed ourselves to forget about the real world. I knew once Dax woke up, we would end up having a quickie before the awkwardness would inevitably settle between us. Neither really knowing what to say. The predictable conversation would follow; we could still be friends, and nothing would change between us, but the words would feel like a flimsy bandage over a gaping wound. I just didn't have it in me to hear them. I couldn't.

So, I packed up my meagre belongings, trying to be as quiet as possible, and was grateful I didn't have much. Most of what I had brought was food, and it was nearly all gone. Dax would have to deal with the rest.

Standing at the cabin door, I wanted nothing more than to return to a sleeping Dax and curl up beside him on the sofa. It had felt like time was standing still as we kissed the night before, creating a memory, a timestamp that would last a lifetime. At least for me, anyway. Dax had made me feel special. The fact he had kissed no one else since that night we met... it had to mean something, right? But in the cold light of day, I knew it wouldn't be enough. The sting of rejection would be bad enough, but coming from Dax, it would have crushed me completely.

"FUCK!" I shout into the cushion, the word vibrating through the fabric. "Why did my heart have to choose him out of everyone? You're so stupid, Tris." For good measure, I give the poor pillow a good whack. Then the tears come as I recall how he held me, the smiles and smirks that lit up his handsome face. The way I had to show him how to make my sandwich. The way he ripped my clothes from my body and fucked me so hard I saw stars. The way his cologne mingled with the scent of his skin, the way his lips felt against mine, soft and warm, and how we lost track of time as we kissed. It's what dreams are made of. And now all of mine are shattered.

"Why him?" I keep asking myself. Choked up, I whisper, "Of all the men in the world, I had to fall in love with Dax." The pain is unbearable, and I cry until I can't anymore. Until sleep takes over.

When I finally get up to use the bathroom, darkness envelops the room. I reach for Dax's cardigan I'd pinched as a memento of our time. Of him. Its familiar texture and scent bring a sense of comfort to the all-too-quiet room. The lingering scent of his aftershave is all that's left, and the memories it triggers cause me to sob uncontrollably. It feels like I've become a master of throwing myself pity parties. Why does it hurt so much? I knew from the beginning that it was temporary, but unexpectedly, everything I'd envisioned for my life began falling into place. As the saying goes, "If it sounds too good to be true, it likely is."

For the next three days, I lie like a dirty slob on my sofa, empty food containers littering the surrounding floor, the scent of my unwashed body hanging heavily in the air. *Eau de Body Odour*. I'm a mess, but I can't even be bothered to care. Ugh, Dax is all I can think about. I'm miserable. I'm drowning in tears, a hollow ache in my chest. Oh, and did I mention that I'm miserable?

Sniffling, I wipe my nose on the cuff of the cardigan, its once-familiar scent of Dax now completely gone. It smells like that Brie I tossed. Stale and mouldy. Like me. My puffy, sore eyes feel raw as another round of tears spills down my cheeks. The guy on TV is showing the proper way to chop wood, and it brings back memories of Dax, causing me to have another emotional breakdown, my 157th to be exact. Then the cooking show featuring Britain's best sandwiches reminds me of Dax and we're cueing 'Emotional Breakdown episode 158.' You get the picture. I'm a train wreck.

The sudden banging on my door makes me jump out of my skin. What in the world? Who's visiting me? Everyone I know will be celebrating with their friends and family, not checking on me. I ignore it, just in case it's someone who goes around looking for sad, heartbroken guys to murder at Christmas! Maybe if I cover my head with the pillow, they'll leave. Or maybe they'll think the house is empty and decide to break in. I don't want to be murdered and end up on one of those true crime shows. The knocking starts again.

"Tristan, if you don't open this door, I swear I'll knock it down myself," a familiar voice threatens. "I know you're in there. I can smell you!"

Jake. Great.

My foot collides with a pizza box, the scent of pepperoni and cheese still lingering. "Two slices left," I muse. "Perfect for a midnight snack."

"Tristan!" he yells. "You have till the count of three..."

Before he can finish, I fling the door open. A look of concern, perhaps even disgust, crosses Jake's face as he takes me in. He looks good. His brown hair, so like his dad's, hangs loosely with a slight wave, reaching just past his ears. He wears a red college hoodie that fits his five-foot-ten frame perfectly. Black *Converse* complement his snug-fitting blue jeans. Jake was always too plain for my taste, but I can see why Lewis is drawn to his fresh-faced, boy-next-door charm.

"Are you gonna keep ogling or let me in?" he says, brushing right past me.

"Well, hello to you too," I say sarcastically. "And *ewww*, I wasn't ogling you." I shut the door and trail behind him.

"What on earth happened in here?" he exclaims, surveying the chaotic scene. "It smells like something died in here. And don't get me started on the state of you right now." Running his hand through his hair, he takes the mess in with a sigh.

"If you're just here to be mean, you can leave." I sink back onto the sofa, crossing my legs, and then my eyes catch a stain on my shorts. It's probably mayo from my lunch. Grabbing a pillow, I plop it on my lap to hide it. I had to change out of my three-day-old sweats earlier because my drink, in a fit of fizzy rebellion, decided to explode all over me. But I'm keeping this cardigan on, even if Jake has to bury me in it.

"I'm not being mean. I'm telling you the truth. And... I was worried about you. Seems my instincts were right," he says as he flicks a takeaway box onto the floor and then sits down beside me.

"Well, as you can see, I'm doing just fine." Crossing my arms, I stare directly into his eyes, challenging him. Jake is my best friend, and he can see right through me. He knows I'm struggling. With a slight tilt of his head and a raised eyebrow, the sympathy in his gaze is enough to send me into another round of tears.

"Shit, come here." In an instant, he sweeps me into his strong arms, his embrace tight and comforting. "What's going on, Tris? Is it your mum?"

"No," I choke out, the sound muffled by my sobs.

"You wouldn't be in this state if it wasn't something bad. I called your phone and left messages. Since when do you not reply to me?"

"I don't even know where my phone is," I tell him. It's likely still in my bags by the door.

Jake squeezes me tight. "Talk to me, Tris. What's going on?"

Releasing him, I bend and snatch a takeout napkin from the floor—it looks mostly clean—and wipe my face. Jake's face twists into a grimace as he looks at me. I know it's pretty gross, but I'm definitely embracing the '*I haven't showered in days*' vibe, so a half-used napkin is practically a spa treatment compared to my current state.

I let out a sigh. I desperately need to talk to someone about Dax, and while I'm not sure if his son is the right person, it's not like I have anyone else. Jake has never judged me in the past, so I just hope he doesn't start now.

"I'm... heartbroken." The knot in my throat tightens as I try to swallow the lump before the tears fall again.

"Heartbroken? How? You've only been to the cabin—" One look at me and the dots must connect. Me. His dad. A cabin... "Oh. *Ohhhh...* You didn't," he says, shaking his head and rubbing his nose with a weary sigh.

"I did," I whisper, my bottom lip wobbling ominously. "I did."

Jake pulls me in for another hug. "Shit, Tris. You had to fall for the one guy who's scared of commitment!"

"You're not upset with me?" I murmur against his shoulder.

He chuckles softly. "No, I'm not upset with you, you dingbat. I knew you liked him, but it's obviously more than just a crush now. I'm definitely taking the award for being the worst friend ever because I should've seen the signs a mile away."

A shared chuckle rumbles through us as we settle back onto the worn cushions of the sofa. "I'm here now. Tell me what happened. Something happened, right?"

I laugh as he rummages around on the floor, his hands moving like he's trying to avoid a contagious disease, finally pulling out a napkin for me.

"Yeah," I nod, letting out a deep sigh of relief. "Something totally happened."

"All right, let's start from the beginning. Tell me everything."

"Well..." I start, but I'm cut off.

"Wait!" Jake stops me with his palm up. "I'm amending '*tell me everything*.' Can you filter some things, please? I do not need to know about my dad's..." He motions at his own groin area. "You know."

I burst out laughing. "Okay, no talking about your dad's dick."

"Tristan!" he shouts, covering his ears.

And so, I spend the next few hours telling my best friend how I fell in love with his dad.

Chapter Nineteen

"Dad?"

"Jake!" I shouted, rushing out of the kitchen where I'd been pacing for hours, desperate for news. "Did you find him? Is he ok? Where is he? What did he say? Oh God, he hates me, right?"

"Calm your tits, Dad. Let's go sit down and I'll tell you." He closes the front door and strides past me like my life isn't in ruins, crumbling around me with every step.

"But is he all right? At least tell me that." I enter the living room behind Jake, but I still can't settle. My anxiety levels are too high, and I just end up pacing around some more, almost ready to wear a hole in the carpet.

"Yeah, Dad, he's fine. Or he's doing as well as he can, considering he's living on takeout and tears."

I pause my nervous pacing to look at Jake, who sits calmly on the sofa. "What does that mean? Is he hurt? Please, Jake. Give me something, anything," I all but beg.

Jake scrutinises me from head to toe, with his brow furrowed in thought. "I didn't realise it was this bad. You're in the same rough shape as Tristan."

You'd feel crushed too, right? The one person who sees through your defences, the one guy who gets you, just leaves. "No... I'm just... a little worried, that's all. It's impossible not to worry when someone leaves without saying goodbye, doesn't leave a note, and then won't even answer my calls. You'd be freaking out too," I murmur.

My son's eyebrows shoot up as he watches me pace again, a look of confusion on his face. "I've never seen you act like this, Dad. It's strange."

"Like what?"

"Worried. No—frantic. Manic, even. I never thought I'd see the day that my dad would fall in love."

Fuck, is that it? My stomach drops. It's too soon to love Tris, but I know that what I'm feeling is very close to it. Stopping in front of my coffee table, I can't take it anymore. I'm overwhelmed. My heart starts racing frantically and I feel sweaty. My hands are shaking. What have I done? What the fuck have I done? The image of a crying Tris, alone in his flat, cold and in a takeout-induced coma, flashes before my eyes. I need to fix this. I need Tris back. I need him to know that those days in the cabin weren't just a fleeting thing to me. That those days were as real as anything has ever felt in my life. Feeling lightheaded, I crouch down, balancing on the balls of my feet, my head dipped low as I try to catch my breath.

"Dad." Jake is by my side in a second, his hand on my shoulder grounding me. "Breathe, Dad. It's okay, I'm here."

"I want him back, Jake," I choke out. Looking up at my son, I croak, "I need him back."

Jake gives me a sad smile. "Let me help you, then. Let's get you on the sofa." He's worried. I can hear it in his voice. I shouldn't have panicked, calling him to ask about Tris and informing him I'd not heard from him in days. But I was at my wit's end, not knowing if he was okay. I don't know where he lives, though. If I did, I'd have gone and broken his door down just to make sure he was all right.

I let Jake pull me up, and we walk to the couch, where I slump down, running my hands through my greasy hair. Showering has not been a top priority over the last few days. I've been wallowing. Miserable. Sad. All the things I've never felt before for anyone other than Jake, invading my body and mind. Every conscious thought has been about Tris.

"Please, Jake, is Tris okay?" I whisper. He takes pity on my pathetic self, squeezing my shoulder as he sits next to me. "Yeah, Dad, he's okay. He's sad and stinks to high hell. But he's okay."

"Why did he not answer his phone? Why did he leave?" Shit, I can feel the tears well in my eyes. How did I become this pathetic guy who thought he could stroll through life one hookup at a time? No care for myself or others, really. All those guys who wanted more with me, I rebuffed, thinking they were just trying to tie me down. But all they really wanted was exactly what I wanted right now. Someone to love and spend my life with. God, I was such a dick. Maybe this is my karma. The universe gave me Tris, then promptly ripped him from me as punishment. And fuck, does it hurt.

"I'm not sure it's my place to fill in all the details."

Sitting up, I grab Jake's hand. "Please. I need your help. I need to fix this."

Sighing, he looks right at me, almost like he's trying to find out if I'm being sincere. I can't blame him, though, because he's grown up knowing I never wanted a partner or any kind of commitment, so why would I want it now? Why would I want his best friend?

"You really like him?" It's a statement, not a question.

"Yeah," I huff. "I *really* do." I smile at him and hope he can see I'm telling him the truth.

"Shit, Dad. I didn't see this coming; I told Tris the same. I should've seen the signs, I guess. The way you two acted on the call. I guess I was so wrapped up in my bubble that I didn't see yours."

"I didn't mean for this to happen, it just did. I mean, I'll admit I've been attracted to Tris since your birthday, but going to help him at the cabin was all I planned on doing. Then the snow started, and Tristan... well, let me tell you, he knows his own mind and isn't afraid to share it." I chuckle. "We had such a great time together. I dunno where I went wrong."

Jake laughs, "Tris is definitely a firecracker when he wants something. But you didn't do anything wrong. He's had it rough over the years and likes to protect himself. He thought you were going to end your little arrangement and tried to save himself the heartache by leaving. Not that it helped him because he's a mess."

"God, he's a pain in my arse. If he'd have just stayed, I was gonna tell him I wanted to see where things could go between us." I let go of Jake's hand and lie back on the sofa, rubbing my eyes. "What do I do, Jake?" I'm so desperate that I'm asking my son for relationship advice. It would be laughable, but I genuinely need his help.

"Tristan needs proof, Dad. Validation he's worth it, and that you want him wholeheartedly. And I also need to know this is not just going to be some fling. Because Tris is my friend and if you plan on dropping him like a hotcake as soon as you get bored or decide a relationship is not for you anyway, then I beg you to just let him go." Jake's facial expression tells me he's dead serious; if I don't man up and give Tris what he needs, he's off-limits.

Sitting up, I face Jake. "I promise you this is not a fling, at least not for me. I really do want to see where this can go with him. If I can convince him to take a chance on a middle-aged schoolteacher. Any ideas on how I do that?" I need a grand gesture, something to show him I mean business. Jake ponders for a minute. If anyone knows how to help me woo Tris, it's Jake.

"Well... New Year's Eve is in a few days and the shelter he works at is having a party. It starts at five, and Tris wouldn't miss it for the world. Maybe you could turn up, see if he'll talk to you?" He shrugs. "Me and Lewis are stopping by. We're donating some sleeping bags."

My son is a good soul. He's going to make a brilliant doctor one day soon and I couldn't be prouder of him. "That's perfect, son. Do you think they'll mind if I turn up?"

"Nah. It's open to the public, too. Not that many people attend the party, but they do donate to the shelter."

Seeing Tris in his work environment—the place he loves so much—would be great. A plan is starting to form in my mind. I've got a few days to pull this off, so I need to get myself together. Tristan Hayes will be mine again... I hope. At the very least, I'm determined to give it my very best shot.

"That's sad, but at least the shelter gets some much-needed supplies."

Jake agrees. "Well, I'll leave you to your planning. I'm off to meet Lewis for an early dinner. You're welcome to join us?" He gets up and walks to the door.

"No thanks, you guys enjoy your meal. I have a few things to sort out."

"Yeah, make sure a shower is one of them!" Jake teases. "Oh, and Dad?" Jake turns to me, looking serious again. "Good luck, and please take care of Tris. Treat his heart as if it's your own." With a pat on my shoulder, he turns and leaves. I lean on the closed door. "I'll do my best, son. I'll do my best."

Chapter Twenty

"*TRIIIISSSSTTTAAANNN.*"

Smiling, I place the tray of mince pies on the snack table for everyone to enjoy. I recognise that sing-song voice instantly. Trixy.

I turn as I watch her walk across the mess hall, the smell of food and the sound of music filling the air as the shelter family celebrates the new year. Trixy wears one of her own knitted hats, the grey of her hair just visible at the bottom, like a hint of the wisdom within. Her long, black winter coat, a gift from me last Christmas, is unbuttoned and flapping in the air as she walks towards me. Underneath is a bright red cardigan, buttoned up to her neck, matching the rosy flush on her cheeks. She has on green trousers paired with purple boots that have seen better days. She's truly a sight to behold! But my favourite part of Trixy is her beaming smile. It lights up her entire face.

When I open my arms out to her, she comes barrelling into me and squeezes me tightly in a hug. "I missed you. I'm so glad you stopped by!" I tell her.

She steps back, her hands resting lightly on my arms, eyes filled with curiosity. "You look different. Spin around, I wanna see you!"

I dutifully spin, my elf hat whirling with me, and it lands over my shoulder as I come to a stop. I decided to hold on to the Christmas cheer a little longer and put on my festive green velour elf outfit, complete with the matching hat. I'm decked out in my red-and-white striped shorts, green knee-high socks that reach just below my knees, and a pair of matching green gloves. My trusty buffalo boots complete the look. As she assesses me, hands on her hips, I hold my breath, anticipating her verdict. After a minute, she tilts her head to the side and smiles knowingly. "You've met someone."

Shit! How does she do that? Her predictions are always spot on; it's almost like she has a sixth sense. I feel my cheeks burning, giving me away completely. A nervous cough escapes my lips as I try to change the subject. "How've you been?"

"Don't '*how've you been*?' me. Answer the question. We're staying put until you give me an answer." With her hands on her hips, she adds a foot tap. There's no way I'm getting out of this.

"Fine. Yes, I met someone, but it didn't work out and I'd rather not talk about it. Sit down, I'll get you something to eat." My voice takes on a sing-songy tone, a playful attempt to divert her attention. "Your favourite item is on their menu. Rhubarb crumble and custard."

"Nice try, kid. Not buying it. But I'll take the pudding. I'm Hank Marvin, and when you get back, you better tell me all about this person."

"Yeah, but..."

"No buts, go get my food. And load it up with custard! The new server guy was so stingy with his portions, you'd think the food was coming straight out of his own pocket!"

I try to hold back a laugh, but a smile tugs at my lips. I'd rather not be on the receiving end of Trixy's wrath, so I do as she says. In the kitchen, I sneak her double portions and then collect the gifts I have for her.

The room buzzes with familiar faces, but a handful of new arrivals also strike me. Their presence always brings a smile to my face—it's heartwarming to see people taking advantage of the shelter. This year, the donations have been truly generous.

Some dance to Jeb's pop playlist on his laptop, but most are just sitting down and eating. I take a seat across from Trixy, pushing the bowl towards her. She eagerly dives into the rhubarb, groaning with pleasure at each mouthful.

"Now, I know you hate getting presents, but I'm gonna give you some, anyway. So here, these are for you." Ignoring her frown, I place the bag on the table. "Whether you open them now or keep them for later is up to you."

She mutters under her breath, but a small flicker of anticipation lights up her eyes as she opens the first gift. Spending money on her makes me happy, even if she doesn't seem thrilled about it. I never had a grandmother, so I think Trixy has become that special person in my life, someone who provides the kind of love and guidance a grandmother would.

"What's this?" she says, pulling out the heat pad from the box.

"It's a heat pad you can rest on your lap, perfect for keeping you warm while you're crafting. Keep those hands of yours nice and warm as well. We need more of your creations," I wink.

She huffs. "Don't butter me up, kid. I'm well aware my work is shit, but it gives me something to do. So, how's this supposed to work? It's not like I can just plug it in."

"It's rechargeable, see?" I show her the charging cable. "You better be in here plugging that in every day, or no double servings for you."

"Spoilsport," she grumbles, but I know she'll do it. "All right, let's get down to business. Tell me all about this new fella you're smitten with."

"What about the rest of your gifts?" She waves me off, her mouth full of crumble, cheeks puffed out. "I'll open those up later. Tell me about your guy. It *is* a guy, right?"

Ha! He's not my anything. I haven't heard from him since the string of frantic messages he left on my phone after I left the cabin. I could have responded to them, but my stupid insecurities held me back, leaving me just rereading them before bed. It was the small reward I gave myself every night for getting through the day. I read them again and again, holding onto the faint hope that he truly cared about me.

I let out a quiet sigh. "Yeah, it's a guy, Miss Nosy." She fixes me with a look that says, *I haven't got all day, get on with it.* "I went to stay at his cabin. By myself," I add as her grin gets wider. "The pipes burst, forcing me to call him for repairs." She wiggles her brows at me, and I can't help but laugh. "A snowstorm hit, making the roads impassable. So, he was stuck there with me."

She leans her head in her hand, completely engrossed in my story. "That's so romantic. Keep going... but skip the steamy stuff. Some of us haven't got lucky in years," she jokes. *Eww,* not a thought I want in my head.

"And then..." she prods.

"And then... nothing. The snow melted, I left, and I've not heard from him since." I don't mention the ache in my heart, the feeling of being utterly shattered, and the way I truly believed I had found my person.

"Hmm. Well, he's either a moron for letting you go, or he's plotting something. I have a good feeling about this, Tris. A little faith goes a long way."

I highly doubt he's planning anything, but as for being a moron, that's on me. Technically speaking, it wasn't him who let me go; *I* was the one who left. Trixy has a good track record, but she doesn't even know Dax, so I'm pretty sure she's missing the mark this time.

Just then, Jake and Lewis catch my eye as they walk in. I wave them over.

"Who you wavin' at?" Trixy asks, turning in her chair.

"My best friend Jake and his fiancé. Be nice," I warn her.

"I'm always nice, you cheeky sod." The smirk on her face tells me she knows just what I'm talking about.

"Mhm," I say, narrowing my eyes at her as I stand to give Jake a hug. "You made it!" I let him go and then hug Lewis.

"Of course we made it. I said we'd be here. You look cute, by the way." He nudges me, giving me a once-over. "Now, who's this pretty lady?" Jake says.

"Oh, he's one of them sweet talkers," Trixy says.

Chuckling, I introduce them all. "Trixy, this is Jake and his partner, Lewis."

"Nice to meet you boys. I hear you're good friends of my Tristan," she says, standing up to shake their hands.

"We sure are," Lewis tells her.

"Well, don't just stand there. You can take me to the food table. I'm starving." I huff as she takes Lewis by the arm and all but drags him to the far end of the hall.

"She seems nice," Jake says.

"Trixy? Yeah, she's a hoot. You might've lost Lewis to her, though." I laugh.

We watch Trixy give Lewis two plates to hold as she stacks them up with food.

"Yeah, you might be right about that." He turns to me. "So, you heard from my dad?"

Shaking my head and crossing my arms, I sigh, "No. But I didn't expect to. It's over, Jake. But I'll survive." I tilt my head up, meeting his gaze, and offer him a half-assed smile. "Honestly, I'm fine. It was fun while it lasted. We were just not meant to be. And that's okay. You don't need to worry about me. Get rid of this." I poke at the frown on his face. "And tell me all about the *fiancé life*."

Jake playfully bats my hand away, chuckling and glancing over to Lewis, making sure his man is okay. It's sweet. When he turns back to me, his eyes are twinkling, and a slow smile spreads across his face. Curiosity sparks in me and I turn to see what's caught his attention.

And... my heart skips a beat.

Dax.

Chapter Twenty-One

MY HEART IS POUNDING so fast it's like a hummingbird trapped inside my chest. Is it possible to explode from the inside out? Because that's how I'm feeling right now. It took twenty agonizing minutes before I could finally pry myself out of the car. When I pulled up, my bravado drained away like air escaping a punctured tyre, and I had to crack the window for a breath of fresh air.

The gentle melody of '*Flaws*' by Callum Scott drifted from the radio as I sat in the car, contemplating the uncertainty of getting out and walking towards what I hoped would be my future. As the song played, I felt Tristan's presence beside me, his words whispering through the music, '*I just want someone to love me, flaws and all.*'

I know I want to be the person who fills that void for him. The mere thought of someone else doing it causes my chest to ache. No, Tris is mine, and I pray to the universe that he feels the same way about me.

As I watched Jake and Lewis disappear through the door, I knew that if I didn't follow them and claim Tristan, my son would feel like I'd let him down as well. I'd also be letting myself down. I've spent years putting the needs of others before my own, but now it's time for me to be a priority.

I carefully pick up the single rose, its petals a deep yellow, perfectly plump like the ones that Tris said his mum loves. My car is also full of backpacks, each filled with necessities for the shelter, but I'll get them later. Right now, I need to go get my man.

Looking at Tristan from the doorway, even with his back turned towards me, I recognise him instantly. Who else would be bold enough to wear an elf costume? Jake meets my eyes and smiles, then Tristan turns, and even from across the room, I can see the startled way he sucks in a breath, his hand flying to his chest like it always does when he's nervous. Taking a deep breath, I walk through the room; the chatter and music around me becoming a dull hum as I focus on him. Tristan gets up, and of course, he's wearing the shortest shorts ever. He's the most adorably sexy elf I've ever seen.

As I stop in front of him, his baby-blue eyes, bright and innocent, look up at me. I'm lost for words, lost in his eyes, as he stares at me, his gaze piercing my soul.

"Dax," he whispers, "W—what are you doing here?"

"I needed to see you," I rasp, my fingers itching to touch him. "Jake mentioned you'd be here tonight."

Simultaneously, our eyes drift to Jake, who's now chatting away with Lewis and a woman wearing a shockingly colourful ensemble topped off with a truly horrendous hat.

"This for me?" he asks tentatively, nodding at the rose.

My focus shifts back to Tris. "Yeah," my voice shakes as I extend the rose to him.

"They're my mum's favourite," he whispers, his gaze watery.

"I remember," I murmur.

"You do?" His face lights up, hope emerging in his eyes.

"Of course I do, Tris."

He leans in close to the flower, his eyes closed as he breathes in its sweet scent. Then, with a dreamy look, he opens his eyes and meets mine. "I love it, thank you. Yellow is also my favourite."

"Tris..." I start. My confidence is wavering again, nerves hitting, but Tris instinctively seems to read me like he always does, reaching out and placing a calming hand on my arm.

"Breathe, Dax," he smiles, and the affection I see in his gaze makes all my doubts wash away in an instant. "Look at me." I do, and everything else bleeds into the background.

It's now or never. The silence stretches as I struggle to find the right words. *Any* words. Tris takes the lead again. "If you and me... If we were a mistake, then just say it, Dax. If you regret it, then tell me. No hard feelings." He blinks at me as he tilts his chin, a newfound determination in his eyes. "But for the record, I don't think it was. A mistake, that is," he whispers. "It *was* a mistake that I left, though. I shouldn't have. That wasn't fair." His bottom lip trembles as he looks around the room. Then he turns back towards me, his hand dropping from my arm. He holds it out in front of me instead, shrugging, trying for nonchalance. "Friends?"

No, no, no! This is NOT going to plan! Everything's going wrong, because I can't get my stupid mouth to work, and my grand gesture is quickly falling apart. Friends, my arse. I'm not backing down this time. I have a purpose for showing up here, and I won't leave until Tris understands my feelings. With a deep breath and a quick unzip, I shed my coat, throwing it over the nearest chair, and exposing the cardigan beneath. *My* Christmas cardigan, covered in Santa's face. I hunted high and low for the ugliest one I could find for this '*Get My Man Back*' mission.

Cupping his chin in my hand, I gently turn his face towards mine, making him look me in the eye.

"I don't regret you or us. Quite the opposite, in fact. If you hadn't stubbornly left that morning, you would have known that. I mean, look at this," I say, motioning towards the cardigan. "I've never really done the festive thing. But I did this just for you."

"For me?" he whispers, furrowing his brow as he takes in the cardigan.

"Yeah. For you, Tris," I tell him.

His hesitant look kills me, but I get it. Trust isn't easy for him, but I'm all in, and now it's time for me to prove it.

"What is it you want, Dax?" he eventually asks.

Taking his hand, I tell him, "*You*, Tris. I want you. I want *us*." I shake my head. "God, these past few days without you... I... I've been fucking miserable, baby. It's like you've put a fucking spell on me. I want you, Tris. Only you."

A subtle smile grows at the corner of his mouth until it blossoms into a full, warm grin. "Really?" he whispers.

"Really—"

"I want you, too, Dax. So much."

Cupping his face in my hand, he leans into the warmth of my touch, his eyes fluttering closed. I lean down and gently brush my lips against his, a soft whisper of affection.

I get lost in his gaze until it dips down, and he takes in the outrageous cardigan I'm wearing. A loud snort escapes his lips. "You really wore that cardigan for me?"

"I did. And don't think I didn't notice my favourite one was gone?" I give him a knowing look.

He tries to hide it, but a delicate tug of his lips and the telltale blush that creeps up his pale neck, give him away. "You can have it, baby. You can have everything I own, as long as I get you in return."

"Dax," he chokes out.

"Wait." Unbuttoning my cardigan, I show him the T-shirt I'm wearing. "Since you love slogan tops so much, I figured I should get one too." I extend the shirt so he can get a good look.

As he reads, tears start streaming down his face. "*Tristan is for life, not just for Christmas.*"

"Too much?" I ask, dropping the shirt, but I get my reply when Tris leaps into my arms. I instinctively catch him, his weight landing on my chest. Legs encircle me tightly, and my hands grip his firm, round butt.

"No, not too much." His warm breath brushes against my neck as he speaks. "Just perfect. I'm sorry I left. I've regretted it every second. I'm such a dumb arse for leaving, but... I just..." he sniffs against my ear.

"I understand why you guard your heart, but you don't have to do that anymore. I'm here now, and I'll protect it for you."

Leaning back in my arms, he looks at me, tears lingering on his eyelashes. "Do you mean that?"

"Yes, little fox. I mean it. I want you, *all* of you. All your imperfections, all your sadness, all your joy. Just please... give me a chance. I know I'm new to this relationship thing, so I'm probably going to mess up sometimes, but I want to try—for us." I'm going all out, leaving myself vulnerable, so he knows I'm 100% in. "What do you say? Do you wanna try forever with me?"

His gorgeous smile, a beacon of light, is all I see as he leans in, his lips meeting mine in a perfect kiss. In front of my son and a room full of people, I kiss the man whose love has woven itself into my heart, one tiny stitch at a time. Tristan's taste is back in my mouth, filling up my half-empty cup till I'm brimming over with sunshine and fucking rainbows.

Pulling back, I ask, "So, is that a yes?"

The sound of his joyous laughter lingers in my ears. "Yes, Dax. All the flipping yeses from here to space and back again." He covers my face with sweet kisses, each one a tiny part of him.

A light tap on my back makes me turn round to see Jake and Lewis grinning at me. "Fucking finally," Jake muses. "So glad you both pulled the sticks out of your arses to figure this out!"

"Heyyy," Tris says, slipping out of my arms, his feet landing firmly on the floor. "It's not our fault it took us so long to get here. Remember your dad's old." He pats my chest with a smirk. The little shit.

I lean in and whisper, "You're gonna pay for that later."

The whimper he gives me makes my dick want to come out to play in the middle of a mess hall full of strangers. Awesome. But I mean what I said. My little fox is going to have to beg for his release later...when he's down on his knees, pleading for mercy.

"Move out of my way. It's my turn to see who this stud muffin is." The rainbow lady, a whirlwind of colour and movement, barrels into the space between Jake and Lewis, halting in front of us. Hand on her hip, she gives me a look that makes me feel like I'm under a microscope, every inch of me being judged. Now, *I'm* the one squirming, and my heart rate picks up a little as I wait for her verdict.

"Is this your guy, Tris? The one you've been pining over?" Straight to the point. No beating around the bush with this lady.

"Yeah, Trixy, this is him. This is my Dax." With a smile, he leans in and kisses my cheek, whispering loudly. "Stunning right?"

"Oh, he's something all right. Tell me, Dax. What are your intentions for my boy here?" Leaning in closer she says, "Now don't bullshit me, son, cos I'll know if you're lying." She waggles her finger in front of my face. I wouldn't want to meet her in a dark alley; she would cut my nuts off and give them back to me as a gift.

I pull Tris closer, holding him tightly against me. I won't lie: I'm using him as a body shield, just in case Trixy deems my answer unsatisfactory and castrates me on the spot. "Well... umm... I want to make sure he's happy and taken care of. To keep him safe and treat him like he's the most important thing in the world." The way he looks at me fills me with a sense of belonging, and I know I'll spend every waking moment cherishing him.

"Leave him alone, Trixy! You've had your fun," Tris laughs.

She pats me on the shoulder with a firm hand. "Yeah, I'm sorry," she chuckles with her raspy voice. "I'm just pulling your leg. Jake filled me in—he mentioned you're his dad." I nod. "I'm trusting you to look after Tristan," she says, her eyes pleading. "He's really special to me."

Okay, maybe she's not as scary as I first thought. "I will. I promise. He's really special to me, too."

She looks back at Tris. "Yeah, this one's a keeper. I like him."

This makes Tris light up. Taking off the hat on her head, she motions for me to put my head down. "Here, this hat is for you. It's a token of my gratitude for loving my boy."

I'm too afraid to say no, so I obey. Dark alleys and my balls in hand come to mind again.

"Thank you," I tell her.

"And don't worry. I don't have fleas; Tris de-loused me last week." She winks.

"Trixy." Tris scolds her just like a grandson would. "Leave him alone, you only had that one flea..."

"What?!" I let out a shriek as everyone bursts into laughter. I'm the butt of the joke, great. I can't do anything about my son teasing me—that's Lewis's responsibility now—but I can teach my little fox a lesson. Later. For now, I playfully pinch his butt and he lets out a screech. The urge to be near him is overwhelming; I'm addicted to him already. Unable to stand the thought of not touching him now that he's mine, I pull him close again.

"Right then, boys, let's go have a little dance. Then I'm gonna need some more food in me soon," Trixy informs us. We all do as we're told. Call us the whipped sheep crew as we '*baaaaa*' along behind her. I, for one, won't be crossing her, that's for sure.

We sway to our own rhythm, ignoring the upbeat music as I hold Tris, clad in an awful cardigan and a hat that smells faintly of... well, let's just say it's seen better days. But I'm exactly where I want to be.

"Looks like Trixy approves of you," Tris comments. "And her judgment of people has never failed before."

"Well, I'm glad because, honestly, she scares the shit out of me."

"She's harmless," Tris chuckles, "but like a grandma to me. Her giving you her hat, she's placing her faith in you. Her trust. It's not just an accessory, but a sign of her expectation that you'll meet her high standards."

"I'm deeply honoured and committed to ensuring I don't let her or you down." I kiss him again just because I can. Because he's mine now. "Thank you for this, for giving us a chance."

"Dax," he coos, his fingers tickling the back of my neck. "I'm just so glad you came to find me. I've been heartsick without you. I was wallowing in my own stupidity." He leans his forehead against mine for a moment, as if recharging himself. When he finally looks up, he says, "No need to thank me either. I mean, you totally can, but I'd rather that you fuck your thanks into me. Hard. All night long."

Fuck! There's my little brat. I'm trying to be all sweet and loving and his mind is in the gutter. I press my semi-hard cock against his belly, and I can tell by the way he licks his lips that he's remembering all the things we did together. "How long till you finish up here?"

"Maybe a couple of hours? Why?"

"Just wanted to know how long I have to wait to be inside you," I smirk.

"Fuck, Dax. That's all I'm gonna be able to think about now while I hand out cookies."

"Good." I give him a quick kiss. "Now, be a good elf and help everyone out while I bring in the backpacks I made." My voice is a low growl next to his ear. "And when you're done, I'm going to take you home and make sure you remember who you belong to."

A whimper catches in his throat, a strangled sound as he bites his lip, trying to hide it. I discreetly ease my hard-on before stepping back from Tris with a wink as I turn, making my way out to the car, a newfound lightness to my step that matches the feeling in my heart.

Chapter Twenty-Two

We scramble toward Dax's car, our haste fuelled by... well, sex! The urge to get naked and make up for lost time consumes both of us. "What's your address?" Dax demands as the car roars to life.

"You wanna come back to mine? Are you sure you don't want to go back to your place?" I suddenly feel a pang of worry, wondering if my rather ordinary apartment will disappoint Dax, who's used to nicer things.

He twists in his seat, pulling me towards him, his lips rough and insistent against mine. The kiss is a primal claim, leaving me breathless and with no doubt about his desire for me.

"I want to be wherever you are," he says, with a hint of possessiveness in his voice. "And I also want to know where you live, so the next time you don't reply to my messages, I can come break down your door."

Jesus, this guy. Let me just take a moment to fan myself. "Kinky much," I snigger. "My place is on Princes Street, the multi-story flats. Third floor," I rush out.

The drive back to my place is quick, taking less than five minutes with Dax behind the wheel. We barely make it inside before he slams me against the wall, his lips crashing against mine in a hungry, desperate kiss. His body feels like granite against mine, the solidity of it squeezing my breath out of me, keeping me trapped. But he doesn't need to worry, though; I'm not going anywhere. We tear at each other's clothes with eager hands, our kisses deepening as we stumble towards my bedroom. Thankfully, I already cleaned the place after Jake's visit, so at least it's clean and tidy. Although the way Dax is consuming me, I doubt he would even notice.

"Wait," I gasp, catching my breath.

"What's wrong?" He frowns at me.

"Nothing, everything's fine, relax. I'm just going to the bathroom real quick."

"Now?" he pants, his chest heaving against mine.

"Mhm. Trust me, you're gonna love it! You'll find the lube in that drawer," I say, pointing to the bedside table as I make my way to the bathroom. "I'll be right back."

Closing the bathroom door with a bang, I rush to my toy cupboard, which also serves as my towel cupboard, and pull out my latest purchase. A tail connected to a butt plug, along with ears on a headband. My pizza-fuelled coma erased all memory of the order, and it arrived yesterday. I didn't think I'd get any use out of it, so I just added it to the rest of my sex toys and costumes. But now things are back on track with Dax, right now, seems like the best time to show it off. Placing the tail and ears on the side of the sink, I reach for some lube from the shelf.

I coat my fingers in the cool gel before lifting one leg up, resting it on the toilet. As I reach behind me and insert two fingers, I bite my lip, closing my eyes and stifling a moan while stretching myself enough to insert the plug. With a few more pumps of my fingers, my muscles start to ease up, signalling I'm ready. I push the cold metal inside slowly, breathing deeply as I feel my arousal intensifying. My cock coming to life.

I brace myself against the sink, allowing a few seconds to let my body settle. I hope Dax likes this gift, since he calls me his little fox. I stand, put on the ears, and then walk back to the bedroom, the tail swinging playfully behind me, brushing against my thighs.

Dax sits at the edge of my bed, holding my dildo in one hand and his erect cock pointing upwards in the other. When he sees me, his menacing growl sends a shiver through my body.

"Is this to your liking, sir?" Slowly, I turn, shaking my tail as I look over my shoulder, meeting his gaze. His eyes are fiery and passionate, voice deep and heavy with arousal as he grits, "Crawl to me, little fox."

So, I do. Getting down on my knees, I crawl on all fours towards him. When I reach Dax, I position myself in the space between his open legs. I'd forgotten just how impressive his beaded cock is—the balls so round and plump. They make my mouth water. A bead of precum sits there, ready and waiting for me. "Please," I whisper, my eyes begging for permission.

"You want this?" he growls, aiming his dick at me.

"Yeah," I say, watching the drop of cum on his tip like it's the only drop of water in a sandy desert.

"Go ahead... lick it."

You don't need to ask me twice. I savour the bitter flavour of his precum as I swipe it with my tongue. I need more, though. So, I swirl my tongue around the head of his cock before moving down the shaft, feeling the beads as they bump across my tongue.

"That's enough. No more for you, greedy boy." His voice comes out stern, and I shiver. "Get on your hands and knees on the bed. I wanna see your tail."

I quickly scramble onto the bed, wiggling my arse excitedly for Dax.

"You did this for me?"

The bed sinks as he settles behind me on his knees. Looking over my shoulder, I groan out a clipped "*Yesss*" in response to his tapping on the plug.

"You really *are* a naughty little fox, aren't you? You want me to fuck you with your tail?"

"God, yes," I whine, chasing his hand with my ass.

"Stretch your arms out straight on the bed and let me get a good look." Once I'm in position, I feel the slight pull as he begins gently sliding the plug out. "Look at that greedy hole, slurping down the plug like you're sucking on Santa's candy cane."

"Aghh," I grunt, as the plug pops out and is quickly jammed back in. Over and over, he teases me. A string of precum marks the bed cover where my cock is dripping. "I need you inside me, Dax," I say urgently.

"If only you'd remembered that when you were acting like a brat at the shelter. You'll only have my cock when I decide you deserve it," he says firmly in his schoolteacher's voice.

I'm gonna die. I'm on the brink of exploding. How will I be able to endure this any longer?

With a knowing smile, he looks down at me. "I have a feeling you can handle even more."

I find a moment of relief as the plug lands next to me, only for his fingers to breach me. It feels like at least two rammed inside me.

"I can't resist you, Tris, the way you tighten around my fingers. Squeezing them. I can't wait to feel you around my cock," he croons. His fingers move around inside me in a circular motion, as if he's trying to polish a doorknob.

"*Daaax, please,*" I whine. Panting heavily, I'm left feeling lost and empty as his fingers pull away from my opening.

"Mmmm. You can definitely take more," he says with a satisfied hum. "I want you to lie on your back for me, baby, so I can see you better. I want to see your tears flow as I wreck you with your dildo."

Fuck. His dirty mouth gives me goosebumps as I roll onto my back. His wild, untamed expression is intoxicating, and I love it. I look up at him with a smile, ready for what's in store. Fingers crossed, it's an epic pounding. Dax lubricates my loyal friend and edges closer to me as I spread my legs. Showing Dax my flexibility, I hook my arms around each of my thighs, baring myself to him. Despite my best efforts, a moan escapes my lips as I'm stretched open once more, the dildo breaching my entrance. Relishing the intrusion, I savour the expression of awe on Dax's face as he watches the dildo disappear inside me. He keeps pushing until I'm completely full, sweat pearling across his forehead.

"So fucking hot. You take this cock so well. How many times have you fucked yourself with this, thinking of me, Tristan?"

"So many times," I admit.

"That's what I thought," he smirks.

The dildo glides in and out of me while I whimper like the needy whore I am. My body thrums with energy, every cell vibrating with the anticipation of an imminent, powerful release. I claw at the sheets, my head spinning wildly, as Dax continues his relentless assault.

"I'm gonna come," I warn him.

Dax comes to a sudden stop, his warm breath fanning my face as he leans down and kisses me. The taste of him, mixed with the salty sweat on his skin, floods my senses as our tongues intertwine. "You will only come when I give you permission, no sooner."

He relentlessly pushes me to the brink of climax, only to pull away at the last moment. My pleas for more grow louder when he pauses, and I instinctively arch my back as he hits my sensitive spot repeatedly. My limbs feel like lead, and I can't keep my legs up anymore. They just fall open onto the bed. He wasn't wrong when he said he was going to have me a crying, sobbing mess. Tears trail down my cheeks, my climax just out of reach. Dax has edged me within an inch of my life. And I wouldn't change a thing!

"You've been such a good little fox. I think you've earned my cock," he praises me, real admiration in his voice, as he pulls the dildo from my pulsing hole.

"Yes... please. I need you. I'm begging you, don't make me wait any longer."

Dax's smile softens, his eyes crinkling at the corners, as he lies on his side next to me. "On your side," he instructs.

I sink into the cool pillow, feeling Dax's hot body against mine and his cock pressing into me as he lifts my leg. At last. My arm curls around his neck as he pushes into me, his pelvis meeting my backside with each thrust.

"Dax... Dax..." I moan. "Just like that. Ugh, your cock is just so... good. Take my arse whenever you feel like it. I'm all yours."

"Promise?" he whispers into my ear.

"I promise."

He rocks into me slowly and steadily, and the beads that line his shaft just hit differently. I tilt my head so that he can kiss me while he buries himself deep within me. His hand gently settles on my stomach.

"Tris, place your hand here. Do you feel me? Feel how far within you I am, deep in your belly."

"Yes, I can feel you. So deep. I want you to fuck me forever, Dax. Never stop."

"I'll fuck you for as long as you want. Always."

"Kiss me and make me come."

The way he kisses me makes me feel like I'm the only person in the world. Working together, our bodies bring us to the edge of release.

"Dax," I whisper. "Can I come?"

"Yeah, baby. Come for me," he urges, his voice low and husky.

That's all it takes. I let go. "*Ahhhhh. Fuucckkkk.*" My body convulses and shakes as pleasure floods through me, as I come hands-free, Dax's cock so deep inside me. "Ohhh... God... Dax..." I cry out.

Cum shoots out of me in abundance, as if it was saving itself for this moment. My body aches in the best of ways. A big, beaded cock attached to a man I thought was unattainable has thoroughly used and fucked me into oblivion.

"You want me to fill you up?" Dax grits, and I can tell that he's close, his sweaty forehead resting against my shoulder.

"Yes, more than anything, please," I tell him. "Give me your cum. I need it."

"Feels like I've waited my whole life to meet you, Tris. You're like a dream. I love being inside you. I'm ready. This is what I want. I want you, us, all of it. Whatever the future has in store, I want it all with you."

My eyes brim with tears as he moves inside me, the sound of our skin meeting filling the room. The sweet, intoxicating scent of us hangs heavily in the air, intensifying with each push and thrust as he drives himself deeper and deeper. A big hand grips my hip, and I hope the bruises will be visible in the morning. His movements become unsteady as his orgasm finally overwhelms him, his cock pulsating as he releases with a deep, drawn-out moan. "Tristan."

His hot cum inside me feels like a satisfying, warm meal. I'm full. At last, I'm full, the void inside me gone. Leaning back onto his chest, we both savour the aftermath of our passion, our bodies spent. Occasionally his cock twitches inside me, pulling small after-shocks from my body before he slips out. We lie there, as the darkness and the quiet envelop us like a comfortable blanket. Neither of us wants to move, but the urge to snuggle wins in the end. Turning over to face him, my lips brush against his in a soft, gentle kiss. Suddenly, uncertainty courses through me, and I squeeze my eyes closed.

"If this is a dream, I don't ever want to wake up again," I whisper. A strong arm snakes around me, pulling me close against a warm chest.

"Open your eyes, baby," Dax murmurs against my lips. I shake my head. I don't think I can. "Tris, baby," he rasps, his voice heavy with emotion. "Don't you dare disappear on me again. Not when I've just got you back. Open your eyes."

Carefully, I blink my eyes open, his honest gaze meeting mine.

"I'm still here, my little fox, and I'm not going anywhere. Not ever. Now sleep, baby. Sleep. When you wake, I'll be here."

Fatigue finally pulls me under, and I'm now filled with a sense of calm. Right now, I feel like I have everything I've ever dreamed of. It's hard to imagine life being much better than this.

The two of us, Dax and I. Me and Dax.
Just Us.

Epilogue

"Are you sure you want to come in?" Tris asks me for the hundredth time, his voice laced with worry, as we get out of my car outside The Willows Nursing Home where his mum is a resident. The crisp air nips at my face as I walk around the car, pulling him close and kissing him.

"I'm certain. Everything will be alright, baby."

"But what if she's having a bad day? I don't want you to hate her if she says something mean. You know she can't help it but..."

To silence him, I press my lips against his once more. The desire to meet the woman who gave Tristan life has been simmering in me for some time. But I didn't want to rush him; I wanted him to feel ready for me to meet her. It breaks my heart to see him arrive home each week, broken and incomplete, because his mother is lost in her own world, ignoring her extraordinary son. I know it's not her fault, and I would never blame her, but I still want to share in his sadness. I need to experience it myself.

"I'm not going to hate her. Fern is an important part of my life now because she's your mum."

His blue eyes glisten before he leans his forehead against mine, letting out a weary sigh. "This is why I love you, Dax." His hand comes to rest on my cheek. "Your compassion and reassurance are like anchors, keeping me grounded when the world feels like it's spinning. I love you so much," he says, his voice filled with warmth and sincerity.

Pulling back, I kiss his forehead. "I love you too, little fox. Please stop worrying. I want to meet her."

"Okay."

"Come on, let's go." I grab the yellow roses from the back seat and take Tristan's hand in mine as we walk to the door. I hold it open for him, and we make our way inside. We're greeted by a friendly lady dressed in navy-blue scrubs. Her broad smile widens when she sees Tris.

"Well, look what the cat dragged in," she chuckles. "And who is this handsome man? Yours I hope?" She winks at me.

"Hey, Denise. Yeah, he's all mine," he beams. "This is my boyfriend, Dax. Dax, this is Denise, Mum's carer."

"Nice to meet you," I nod.

"You too, Dax," she smiles.

"I'll sign us both in and grab lanyards," Tris says to me. Turning to Denise, his voice takes on a sad tone as he asks, "How is she?"

Denise's smile never falters as she pats Tris on the shoulder. "Go see for yourself."

With the visitor lanyard around my neck, Tris takes my hand. I squeeze it reassuringly as we walk towards an open door. The room is a large living room, overflowing with comfy armchairs, some occupied by residents while others are vacant. The room is brightly lit, painted a cheerful apple green, and adorned with colourful pictures on the walls.

Standing with her back to us at the far end of the room, a woman in a dark green cardigan and black trousers seems to gaze out at the garden beyond the French windows. Her red hair, as vibrant as autumn leaves, flows freely down her back, cascading to her waist. With a shared glance, we both walk toward her.

"Mum," Tris speaks softly. "It's me, Tristan."

It feels like a sharp, piercing stab to my heart to think he has to introduce himself to his own mother. The lady glances over her shoulder, and then a wide, radiant smile spreads across her face. With slow movements, she turns to face us. "Tristan, my boy. Come, give me a hug," she says, opening her arms wide.

Tris halts abruptly, a hand flying to his chest, his breath hitching in his throat. He wasn't expecting his mum to acknowledge him, let alone recognise him. Her words clearly catch him off guard since he has grown accustomed to her dementia and has come to accept that he will never get his mum back. I know what this moment of recognition means to him.

"Mum," he murmurs softly, releasing my hand as he moves toward her open arms. Seeing them together makes me tear up. I'm happy I got to witness this special moment.

"There, there, my darling. I've missed you. I feel like we haven't seen each other in a very long time," she tells him while gently rubbing his back. Her eyes, bright and curious, flick up to meet mine. "Oh Tris, you brought your husband with you today," she exclaims.

Tris stands back, a hand coming up to wipe his eyes before looking at me.

"Oh no, Mum, he's not..."

"Hello, Fern. How are you doing today?" I cut him off mid-sentence as I step forward and give her a kiss on the cheek.

"I'm feeling fantastic now that you're both here. Are these for me?" Her head dips in a nod towards the roses.

"Yes, I heard these were your favourite." I wink at Tris, trying to lighten the mood as he gathers himself.

"Indeed, they are. I love them. Thank you so much. Did you get them from Harry's? His are the best in town, and he knows exactly how I like them."

"We did, didn't we, Tris?" I give him a reassuring smile. Leaning in closer to Fern, I near-whisper, "Your son even showed me how to pick out the best ones." I subtly tap my nose, as if sharing a secret only we know.

She whispers back conspiratorially, "The squeeze test. It's the only way." We share a laugh together.

"There you go, folks! Tea for everyone," Denise announces, as she sets a tray on the side table. "I'll leave you to it."

"Shall we sit?" I suggest. With a nod, Fern settles into her chair, placing the flowers beside her as Tris and I pull up a chair. "You good?" I mouth to him. He responds by offering me a watery smile, and my arms itch to just wrap him up in a hug. My poor baby.

Once we are all settled and Fern has her tea in hand, her curious gaze meets mine.

"I'm really sorry, but I don't remember your name, love. My brain isn't always as sharp as it could be."

"That's okay. I'm Dax."

"Dax, that's it. Now I remember. Silly me." She chuckles to herself. "I remember your wedding; it was in the spring, and the foxgloves on the tables made everything smell amazing. The ceremony was beautiful. You made my Tris smile ear to ear that day."

Tristan's hand trembles in mine, and I hear the ragged sound of his breath as he fights to compose himself. Since we are not married, there has been no wedding or ceremony. Not yet, anyway. It wouldn't be fair to spoil things for her, though, so I happily play along. Fern clings to a memory that she believes is true and maybe, one day, it will be. If it's up to me, it definitely will.

"I agree with you, Fern. It was a beautiful day, and I'm the lucky one. My life is perfect now that I have Tristan. Thank you for bringing up such a kind and generous man." I gently press a kiss to the back of his hand.

"He was born with a kind soul, not a bad bone in his body," she agrees affectionately.

The love in her eyes for her son is clear, a warm glow that lights up her entire face. The moment might be fleeting for her, but it's undeniably present for both of us to witness. I understand today is a good day for Fern, and it might be some time before Tris has the chance to see his mother like this again. My boyfriend is clearly emotional at the moment, but I want to make this visit so special that he'll remember it on his tough days.

The ring in my pocket has been my constant companion for the past month. I know it sounds strange, but when I passed by the jewellery store and saw it, I just had to have it. It was a beautiful sight and reminded me of Tris, so I stepped inside the shop and bought it without a second thought. It's still early in our relationship, but today, with his mum in high spirits, it feels like the perfect time to give it to Tris.

I want Tris to know that I care for him deeply, and I want to share this moment with his mother so she can feel the love I have for him. She may not remember it tomorrow, but Tristan will, and I'm determined to give him that memory. "Hey Fern, I was wondering if it would be okay if I gave Tristan a little something?"

"I think that's an excellent idea," she says, nodding in agreement.

Turning to Tris, he tilts his head, a bewildered expression on his face as his eyes dart back and forth between me and his mother. Dropping to my knees in front of him, I make sure we are both in his mum's line of sight.

"What are you doing?" he murmurs, his bottom lip trembling.

Leaning in, I brush my lips against his in a quick, light peck, taking both his hands in mine. "Tristan, I know we're already married." I give him a knowing wink. "But I wanted to give you this gift to represent my promise to you. Ever since the day I saw you at Jake's birthday, you've been running circles in my mind. Never did I think the day would come that I could make you mine. But here we are."

"Dax," he whispers, his voice shaking.

Pulling out the black velvet box, I turn it around, the weight of it heavy in my hand, and open it, revealing to Fern the gift I've chosen for her son.

"Beautiful," she sighs, instinctively placing a hand on her chest, just like Tris always does. I turn back to him, opening the box, revealing the silver band with a bright yellow stone nestled in its centre. His hands shoot to his mouth, stifling a gasp, and his eyes dart to me, as they well up with tears.

"What did my shirt say again? Oh yeah, Tristan is for life, not just for Christmas. What do you say, little fox? Will you be mine forever?"

Laughter bursts from my lips as Tris crashes into me, sending me tumbling backward. His kisses and tears rain down on my face, leaving me breathless and with no doubt that I've made the right decision.

"So, does that mean yes?" I ask as I kiss him back.

"Yes, yes, yes. All the yesses in the world."

"We better get up before they kick us out," I tell him, giving him a quick kiss as we lie on the carpeted floor of the nursing home.

"Oops," he says with a sheepish smile. Offering Tris my hand, I help him back to his feet.

"Put it on me," Tris says, his fingers wiggling impatiently in front of me, his smile growing wider by the second.

I pop the box open again, the velvet lining giving a soft snap, and slide the ring on. It isn't a perfect fit, feeling a little loose on his finger, but I was acting on instinct when I bought it.

"Let me see," Fern says, rising slowly to her feet. Tris, radiating pride, offers his hand to his mum. "Oh goodness. It looks even better on your finger!" she exclaims.

Since she already believes we're married—and it sounds like Fern truly believes we had a beautiful wedding—this is just a little something extra for my 'husband,' or, I suppose, my now fiancé!

"I can't believe it," Tris says incredulously. "Are you absolutely sure? Don't you think it's too soon?"

I pull him toward me, captivated by the light dancing in his sapphire eyes, and whisper, "Tris, I've never been surer of anything in my life than I am right now. Apart from Jake being born, this is the best day of my life, and I'm determined to create many more days, just like it." With him, I feel like I can finally breathe and be myself. Before him, there was a void, and after him, there will be nothing but memories. The remnants of his tears still glisten on his cheeks. "There's only one thing I need from you, Tris," I say.

"What's that?"

"To be with you forever, little fox. My heart belongs to you, and I promise to love you until my last breath."

Tears stream down his face as he hiccups. "I want that too, Dax. So much."

I've made a solemn vow to my man in the presence of his mother, and I'm fully committed to keeping it. Mr. No-Commitment just broke his own rules... again!

THE END

Chit-chat and Playlist

Did you like *A Crush for the Holidays*? Reviews from readers like you help indie authors get noticed, so if you liked this book, please consider leaving a review on goodreads, The StoryGraph, Amazon, or wherever you shop for books.

Thank you for reading!

Turn the page to see the music that motivated me while I was writing *A Crush for the Holidays!*

Curious about the music that inspired me? Want to listen to what Tristan did?
I put together a playlist for that!

A Crush for the Holidays Playlist

Flaws by Calum Scott
this is what slow dancing feels like by JVKE
When Christmas Comes Around by Matt Terry
Snowman by Sia
Dance With You by Brett Young
A Lot More Free by Max McNown
One More Sleep by Leona Lewis
Winter Wonderland by Tony Bennett
All I Want for Christmas Is You by Mariah Carey
Let It Snow! Let It Snow! Let It Snow! by Frank Sinatra
White Christmas by Michael Buble (with Shania Twain)
Mistletoe and Wine by Cliff Richard
Only Thing I Ever Get For Christmas by Justin Bieber
Christmas Love by Ashanti
Merry Christmas by Ed Sheeran and Elton John
Merry Christmas Everyone by Shakin' Stevens
Lonely This Christmas by Mud
Mistletoe by Justin Bieber
Underneath the Tree by Kelly Clarkson
Santa Tell Me (Naughty Version) by Ariana Grande
O Christmas Tree by Teddy Swims
Always Remember Us This Way by Lady Gaga
Little Bit More by Suriel Hess

Home for the Holidays

Acknowledgments

First, I want to give a shout-out to Jay Leigh, who asked me if I'd like to join in with this holiday collection. Imagine lil' ol' me being asked to join with lots of other authors! It made my little indie heart happy. Jay and Dallas's organisational skills are top-tier and made everything so easy for my messy mind to understand. If you haven't checked out the queer collection of books, then now is your chance to pick up some great reads. You can find the full list on the '*Home for the Holidays*' page… which should be before this page. After this page? It's somewhere in this book!

Next is the company I keep. I say it always, but I really do have the best people around me. Jenn is like a more organised version of me. It's like she's inside my brain and goes around with her dustpan and brush, cleaning up all my chaos! She does so much for me behind the scenes, so when it came to picking the date for release, it was a no-brainer to pick her birthday. Thank you, Jenn, for everything you do for me and for having conversations with me just through GIFs!

Anja, of course, is my kinkster-sister co-writer, but she's also a great friend to me. She's a permanent passenger, riding on the hot mess express that is me! She alpha reads my books and is a huge supporter of my guys. She sends me funny memes to keep me going and listens to my voice notes full of all my jumbled ideas before reciting them back to me in a way that makes sense! I couldn't do this author thing without her.

As always, my PA, Marianne, shares the shit out of my books, always on hand to shout at me to *'go write!'* when I'm procrastinating! She's one of my biggest supporters. Thank you for always listening to me and loving my guys.

Regitse, you are new to our crazy crew and a welcome addition. Thank you for all the art you create for us. I love how you're able to capture my guys with just a few details. If anyone needs an artist, then definitely drop her a DM.

A dear friend suffered a loss this year, something none of us want to go through, but even through her pain she checks in to see how I'm doing, and I will forever be grateful for her friendship.

I have a kick-arse street team who also posts the shit out of everything thrown at them. Without them, all my books would get lost in the abyss of book releases, so thank you for giving this indie author a chance to share her men.

Thank you, reader and fellow lover of romance books, for picking up my or any indie authors' books. It really means the world to us when you take the time to read words we have poured many hours into, leaving us reviews so that others might enjoy our words too. Without you, our amazing readers, we wouldn't have books.

This year has been a tough one for my family, with mental health being a very big factor, but having great support around me really does make all the difference. I pray next year brings some good things our way.

I always try to put a bit of myself into my books, and this time I shared dementia. My nan was diagnosed four years ago, and it's hard to see someone who had such a big impact on my life slowly lose herself. But I know I'll always have the memories of my childhood and the time spent with her, and will treasure them forever.

My husband is my rock and supports me even on the bad days. He continues to make me coffee at 11 pm so I can keep working and buys me flowers when he knows I need a little pick-me-up. Here's to another twenty-four years of him putting up with my bullshit!

If I've left anyone else out, you can just blame the ADHD. Please know how thankful I am to have you in my life.

Stay safe and be kind to each other,
Emma xx

Also by E.L. Ough

Christmas in Heaven

(Part of *Kinked for the Holidays* co-written with A.E. Jensen)

Taming Tyler

(Part of *Kinked for the Holidays* co-written with A.E. Jensen)

His Guiding Light

(*Hope Harbour Book 1*)

After the Flames

(*Hope Harbour Book 2*)

Violence & Virtues: Vol. 2

(*A Mafia Romance Anthology* February 2025)

About the Author

Emma is a wife and mum of 4. She lives in the UK where it rains 80% of the year! She's an avid MM reader and a big supporter of the LGBTQIA+ community.

She's a big lover of Christmas, so it's fitting that the first book she wrote was a spicy Christmas novella!

She can usually be found rocking in a dark corner after she's dealt with her kids all day, *hehe*.

Once she's been caffeinated in the mornings, you'll find her reading or tapping away on her laptop—making edits, lengthening the plot bunnies in her head into more stories, and posting about her favourite authors on *Bookstagram* as **@emmareads40**

.

15115744R00104